REMEMBERING TOMORROW

SPECULATIVE STORIES OF THE PAST & THE POSSIBLE

NAOMI ARTEMI

AUGUSTO LUIZ FACCHINI

DEVIN HUNT

C.H. SCOTT

XINYUAN SHI

KEEGAN YOUNG

INK ALCHEMY
BOOKS

Compilation copyright © 2026 by Ink Alchemy Books

Trade Paperback ISBN: 979-8-9906798-7-0
eBook ISBN: 979-8-9906798-8-7

Library of Congress Control Number: 2025922158

Cover Art by Seed Bomb
seedbombpa.com

ANTHOLOGIES ALSO
BY INK ALCHEMY BOOKS

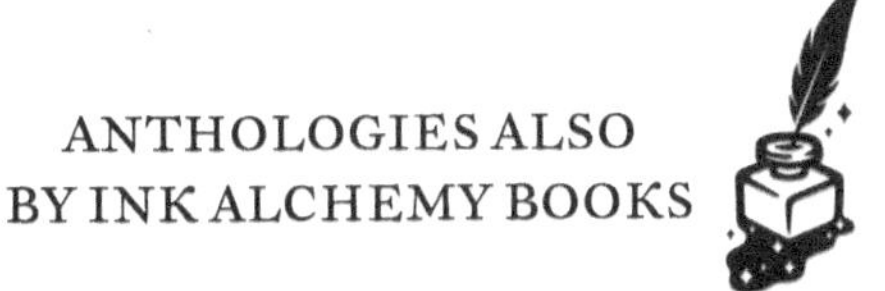

Weirdscapes: An Otherworldly Anthology, 2025

Whimsy: A Literary Doom & Gloom Antidote, 2025

Shift: An Anthology, 2024

Beware the Light: An Anthology of Dark Fiction, 2024

For Meghan,
the Master Mender
—NAOMI ARTEMI

Hold all you love close.
Life's better that way.
—DEVIN HUNT

For those who know
French toast is an anytime food.
—C.H. SCOTT

For the best
librarian I know.
—XINYUAN SHI

For Grandma,
now you're one with the stars.
—KEEGAN YOUNG

CONTENTS

A LIBRARIAN'S MEMORY

XINYUAN SHI

What is a photographic memory? Also known as an eidetic memory, it is the ability to recall a passage or an image with precision after seeing it only once. At least, that is what they would have you believe.

- Broadcaster Anchore, released March 22, 970 Y.A.

Sulivena Smith, known to her friends as Sully, was cleaning the shelves of her beloved library when the bell rang. It was a slow day, and she had sent her assistants, Davina and Puren, home in the morning, so she was the only one left in the building to answer the bell. She left her cleaning supplies in the aisle labelled *Military History* and headed toward the front desk.

On her way, she passed *Art History, Biographies & Memoirs, Religion, Philosophy, and The Arts.* Sully could navigate the stacks in her sleep, and she knew the contents of their shelves as well as the words inside better than she knew the back of her hand. She was the library's librarian, and as such, she had a photographic memory.

The young man at the front desk was a stranger. Dressed in the bold palette of a Language and Culture University student, he had the same expression on his face that all newcomers to the library had—a mixture of awe and incredulity.

"Hello," she greeted him and watched with mild amusement as he jumped in surprise.

"Oh gosh—hello!" The man's eyes met hers. Brown eyes. Long lashes. White, straight teeth. Tan. Prominent brow. Unwrinkled. Curly, black hair. Sully noted each detail mechanically and committed them all to memory. Even if she never saw the young man again until her deathbed, she would instantly recognize him.

It was a charming face—she thought offhandedly.

"Sorry to surprise you. Welcome to the Touchstone Library. I am Librarian Smith. How can I help you?"

"My name is Moar Schitte. I'm an LCU student in the Communications Department, and I would like to interview you for my thesis. Do you have some time today? I could come back if now isn't a convenient time."

Sully was not surprised by the request. As the local librarian, she often received interview inquiries from LCU students aspiring to one day be librarians themselves. Little did they know, becoming a librarian had nothing to do with what courses one took at university, but one's ability to memorize the written word. After all, the people's shared history and memory were stored in libraries, but books and paper were notoriously vulnerable to mold, moths, and fire. If a book were to be destroyed by one of the three, it was the librarian who would immediately work on its replacement, lest its contents be wiped completely from the People's memory.

She decided to humor Moar's request. It would be a welcome break from cleaning. "You caught me on a slow day. I'd be happy to answer some questions. Let's use my office. My new chairs were just delivered, and you can be the first one to test them."

"Thank you!" His smile was broad and bright. Sully spared a thought for all of the broken hearts left in its wake.

"This way," she said. Moar followed close behind as she led him back through the stacks. Touchstone Library was a metropolis filled to the brim with bookshelves acting as skyscrapers and aisles forming entire neighborhood blocks dedicated to a sole subject. A newcomer could get hopelessly lost among the stacks, but luckily for Moar, he had Sully to guide him to the back and towards an inconspicuous door the same gray as the walls.

Sully lifted the lanyard of keys around her neck, selected the right key, and opened the door. Inside was the staff lounge space, made cozy and inviting by Davina's touch and Puren's coffee bar. Sully was very thankful for her assistants and their sense of style. She herself was a utilitarian person—her brain a maze of sentences, paragraphs, and chapters that left little room for superfluous things like decorations unless, of course, she was reciting a book on interior design.

Passing the door to her residential suite, they reached the

back of the lounge space, and Sully opened her office door for Moar. "Make yourself at home," she said and added as an afterthought, "Would you like some coffee or something?"

"I'm good. I had a big breakfast this morning, and coffee after eleven keeps me up far too late." Moar settled into the cushioned armchair in front of her desk. "If it's all the same to you, I'd like to start the interview."

"Alright," she said, making herself comfortable behind a desk full of her latest project—a series of deteriorating biographies on Amnesty's first president, Betulin Angore. She moved a couple of volumes to the floor so she could see Moar better. "What's your first question?"

"Can you tell me a little bit about yourself and this library?"

"My name is Sulivena Smith, and I am the resident librarian of Touchstone Library where we house 54,451 texts written from the Year of Amnesty 467 to present day. We do specialize in topical history with 30,451 works on military history, geological and scientific history, presidential biographies and autobiographies, religious history, governance documents, and political treatises. Other sub-categories include the arts, philosophy, and ethics with 8,421, 4,359, and 4,117 texts, respectively. Collectively, our library and I store over six billion of the People's words. I have been the librarian here for over twenty-seven years now, starting my apprenticeship under my predecessor, Jules Biblio, in the fall of Y.A. 938."

"Twenty-seven years? You hardly look over thirty-five."

Had that been a compliment? Sully ignored it as she continued her recitation. "In that time, we have served over fifty thousand patrons, three presidents and their advisors, seven generals, and six major universities. This library is at the heart of the Inter-Library Loan Network where patrons are allowed access to any resource in the Republic of Amnesty's greater collection. Finally, I have personally been interviewed by a dozen other students such as yourself."

Moar blinked. "That was thorough."

Sully said, proudly, "As thorough as only a librarian can be."

"I'm beginning to see that. I like the introduction, but I'm curious about how *you* became a librarian. You're a Smith, and I thought only Biblios became librarians."

"A common misconception. While that family tends to produce individuals with excellent recall, the only real requirement to become a librarian is a photographic memory. Furthermore, times are rapidly changing, and with the rise of universities, young people have more opportunities to pursue professions outside of their family's trade. Your name, Schitte, is another form of waste. Are you planning on becoming a waste manager?"

"Not if I can help it," said Moar, fiercely. In her brief interaction with the young man, Moar had been nothing but cheerful and charming. Seeing the glint in his eyes, Sully wondered if that had all been a veneer. "Why is a photographic memory vital for a librarian?"

"Do you know the adage, 'The People's identity lies in their memory. Their memory is stored in the library'?"

Moar nodded.

"Well, there's a third line. 'And the library's guardian is

its librarian.' It may seem as if our profession is nothing more than the care of old books, but the founders of our Republic have decided to store our collective memory and knowledge in this library and others like it. Each sentence preserved in these books delineates a historical fact." Sully tapped the remaining stack of biographies on her desk in emphasis. "But our founders were wise enough to acknowledge the fallibility of paper and ink. That's where librarians come in. We need a photographic memory to ensure that each word is preserved the same as the day it was written down by the recordkeepers. Anything less would alter history."

"So, it's true then? We would remember things differently if the books in this library were to change."

"In theory, yes, but in reality, they will never change. Books might be added to the library as current events are recorded, but that is all. We do not allow books to ever leave the premises, and any volume handled by a patron onsite is examined for alterations by my assistants or I before it is returned to the shelf. I take my job very seriously. You're not taking any notes."

"I have a decent memory myself," Moar said.

"Oh?" Sully decided to test him. "How many texts are housed in this library?"

"54,451."

"From what years were they written?"

"That's easy. From Y.A. 467 to the present day."

"Not bad." She nodded with grudging admiration. "Maybe you have a future as a librarian."

Moar laughed. "And waste this face on the stacks? I don't

think so. I've got other things in mind."

"Do you have any other questions?"

"Only one. Could I come back once a week to interview you further? I think your answers will be vital for my thesis."

"Weekly is too much of a time commitment."

"What about biweekly?"

Sully considered Moar and his eager smile for a moment. Like all things, she remembered clearly what it had been like to be a student. Becoming a librarian had been everything to her. Other paths had been unthinkable, failure never an option. And at the end of four long years, it had all culminated in that final thesis. "What are you trying to do with your thesis?"

"Oh, nothing much but change the world." Moar chuckled and shook his head. "No, I'm just trying to graduate with honors. I don't have the memory to be a librarian, but I think a final thesis that dives deep into the merits of Amnesty's libraries and collective history will open doors with policy makers. My dream is to one day work for a think tank and act as an advisor for our government officials."

"That's ambitious."

"What? You think it's too ambitious for a Schitte?" Moar's smile turned bitter.

"Not at all!" Sully, a Smith serving as a librarian, was hardly one to judge. "I've just never had a political studies student interested in the library before. Much less one who wants to base their thesis on it. They're usually far more concerned with current events."

"You're the one who said that libraries store our history.

What would our present be without the past? If nothing else, my thesis will stand out."

Sully could hardly argue against that. "Alright, I'll meet with you every other Thursday. Those are usually our slow days, and I think I could spare an hour. I'll let my assistants, Puren and Davina, know. If you don't see me, one of them will be manning the front desk. They'll let you into this office."

"Thank you." Moar reached out to shake her hand, then meeting her eyes, said, "I won't disappoint."

Those with photographic memories often find themselves in the profession of librarian. Our founders, through no participation of We the people, decided upon the founding of our great republic to store our collective memory in libraries across the country. Librarians were entrusted to preserve that history if anything were to happen to the contents of a library.

I propose that this was a mistake. Librarians are just as human and fallible as the rest of us. They would have you believe that their memory is infallible, so you don't question. They would have you believe that what they're preserving is unaltered history.

There is no such thing.

- Broadcaster Anchore, released May 6, 970 Y.A.

Davina was good-naturedly arguing with Sully at the front desk, trying to convince her mentor of the merits of color coordinating books on their shelves to maximize their aesthetic appeal, when Moar next arrived at the library. Organizing volumes by anything short of the Linnaean system was a preposterous idea, thought Sully. After all, what was the point of aesthetic appeal when patrons were unable to locate a text? Once stuck on an idea, Davina was not one to let it go easily though and suggested that they could try it first with books that were less important. To which, Sully responded with finality that every book in the library was important and turned to address Moar.

He must have had time to change after class that day as he was no longer dressed in the bold palette of an LCU student and was instead wearing a plain short-sleeved shirt and sweatpants. Judging by the way that Davina ogled him, she was no longer thinking about aesthetic appeal—at least when it came to books—Sully thought with amusement.

"Good day," he greeted them with a huge smile. "How are you two doing this beautiful afternoon?"

"Same old, same old," Sully said. "Davina, this is Moar Schitte. He's the student I was telling you about. He'll be here every other Thursday for—" She paused, realizing that she didn't remember the length of their agreement, and turned to Moar. "We never established a timeline for your project."

"Just a few months, at least until the semester ends," he supplied. Then, holding out a hand to Davina, said, "It's a pleasure to meet you. You must be one of the brilliant assistants that Sully mentioned." That was funny—Sully didn't remember mentioning Davina's or Puren's brilliance in their last conversation.

"It's a pleasure to meet you," Davina beamed, shaking his hand.

"Now that the pleasantries are over, let's do the interview in my office again. Davina, are you good at the front desk for an hour? Puren's in the stacks. If it gets busy, call him," said Sully.

"Mmhmm," mumbled Davina. She was still beaming at Moar's back when Sully turned and led him to her office once again.

"Do librarians typically have two assistants?" he asked along the way.

"Yes, Puren is my oldest assistant. He's been with me for five years now. Davina is relatively new and has been here for two years." Sully opened her office door and, rounding her desk, settled herself comfortably in her new office chair. The chairs were by far the best purchase she had made this year.

"How long is the assistantship?"

"Ten years."

Moar whistled. "That's a long time."

"Well, how long would it take you to memorize the contents of an entire library?"

"*Wow.*"

Sully nodded. "It's a long process, but it is necessary to turn someone with potential into a librarian. After all, our value to society is the contents stored inside our brains."

"Do they get breaks?"

"Of course. They get just as many vacation days as any other assistantship and unlimited sick days."

"Are they both Biblios?"

Sully frowned. Moar was far too caught up on the antiquity of family names and their meanings. "Puren is, but Davina is a Miller. Not that it matters. Both have the aptitude to be a librarian, otherwise they would not be my assistants."

"Will they take over this library from you after their assistantship ends?"

"Puren is a good fit and will be the next librarian after me. Davina hasn't decided yet. She is only in her second year. Assistants are typically chosen in their third year and dedicate themselves to memorizing their library's contents."

"What do you mean by chosen?"

This was Moar's hardest question to answer by far. How did Sully describe the sense of a library to someone who only saw it as shelves of old books? That feeling of a massive building welcoming you home? The whisper of ancient stones? The satisfaction of a master key slipping into your hand, the only one it belonged to, and the benediction of texts written before their time but familiar as old friends? Libraries had personalities, and they chose their librarian, not the other way around. When the time came, Davina would know exactly where she belonged.

Sully did her best to describe that ineffable feeling, but she could tell that Moar did not understand. He spent the rest of their session asking her about the mechanics of her memory—a topic that Sully found much easier to describe—and soon their hour was up. Sully escorted him out of the stacks, and he left with a parting, "See you next time." On her way back to her office, she was waylaid by Puren and Davina.

"Who was that?" Puren asked.

"Moar Schitte," Davina answered for her, "He's the LCU student interviewing Sully. He's going to write his thesis on the Library. Isn't that great?"

Sully nodded.

"What's so great about it?" Puren frowned at Davina. "It's just an undergraduate thesis."

"Based on our library! I think it's brilliant to include first-person testimony from Sully."

"Brilliant?" Puren scoffed. "Hardly. You're just saying that because he's easy on the eyes." *Oh Puren*, Sully wanted to shake her head. He had been infatuated with Davina since she had first let loose her dazzling smile upon him. Unfortunately, Puren was much better with books than he was with people, and his crush often showed itself in criticism when a kind word would have been much more effective. As a matter of fact, Sully remembered being like Puren when she was young, but the years had mellowed her.

Perhaps, their library had a type.

Never one to let Puren keep her down, Davina responded, "Oh, isn't he just so *dreamy*?" She let out a sigh. "Those curls! Those muscles! Those *eyes*! I could melt into them like milk chocolate on a hot day."

Puren scowled. "You're too much."

"I know, but you love it."

Seeing that she was no longer needed here, Sully left her assistants to their banter.

"How does the library work?" asked Moar.

In a change of scenery, Sully had decided to simultaneously give Moar a tour of the library while answering his questions.

They were at the furthest end of the *Philosophy* section, and Sully was running her fingers fondly over texts that detailed the lives of the ancient philosophers. "What do you mean?"

"The whole having our memories reflect what's stored in the library." Moar pointed at a volume next to his head. *Formative Events of Lirioden's Youth and the Foundation of Perennialism.* "That book on Lirioden. I doubt that I remember things as clearly as you do, but I know the basic facts of his life. Yet, I don't remember ever reading or hearing about Lirioden before. How is that possible?"

"I'm not sure." Sully shrugged. "The Founders decreed that it would be this way, so it is. Maybe it's in the stones."

"Don't you think that's odd? You're the librarian here. Shouldn't you know how the library fundamentally functions?"

Maybe it was the influence of the texts around her, but Sully found herself suddenly quite philosophical. "Does the bird know how it flies? No, it flies. Does the dolphin know why it swims? Of course not, it's born knowing how. It must in order to survive. I think we librarians are similar. I always knew that I was going to be a librarian, and once I became one, I knew my function was to preserve these books. I never questioned how the library worked. It just does. It has always been this way."

"Hmm." Moar frowned.

"What?"

"I think that's the first time you haven't really answered my question."

"I'm sorry, you asked a tough one," she said.

"Well, then let me ask another one."

"Keeping me on my toes, aren't you?"

"Do you think it's dangerous to have all of our history lie solely in libraries and the memories of librarians? I know you have a photographic memory, but aren't you just human at the end of the day? And last time I checked, people are pretty fallible."

Moar, as Sully had come to learn through his questions, was much more complicated than the charming student that had been her first impression. In front of Davina and even a surly Puren, he was always quick with a smile and a joke. Most of the time with Sully, he was the same, but every once in a while, he would ask her a question that made her wonder. She shook her head firmly. "No, I don't. Ink and paper are fallible. My memory is not."

"Fine, maybe your memory won't ever fail, but you're still flesh and bone. Accidents happen all the time. What happens to the library if something happens to *you*?"

Librarians tended to live long lives, ensconced in the endless stacks of their beloved libraries. What could happen to them? Die under a mountain of books? Sully thought that was just as likely as she was to be forgetful. "What, are you planning something dastardly?"

Moar put a hand to his chest and turned his head in feigned disappointment. "Drat, you caught me."

"All jokes aside, Puren's memory is just as sharp as mine. By the time he finishes his assistantship, he will have the entire contents of Touchstone Library captured in his memory. I will live a very long life, but should anything happen to me, he could replace me in a heartbeat."

"So, your assistant is the backup to the backup?"

"In a manner of speaking, yes." Though, Sully doubted Puren ever thought of himself as such.

"Has it ever happened that a library is left without a librarian?"

"Not that I know of. The Librarian Consortium ensures that each library is occupied by at least one sitting librarian and an assistant with the necessary qualifications."

"Consortium? What a fancy term."

With a straight face, Sully said, "We thought it sounded better than 'a gaggle of librarians.'"

"'A mob of librarians?'"

"We're not gang members. That's much too threatening."

"I got it!" Moar snapped his fingers. "'A stack of librarians.'"

Shaking her head, Sully laughed. "They should have had you on the board."

Think about it.

If you were a librarian and had all this power over the People's history, wouldn't you change things to favor yourself? Wouldn't you manipulate history to convince everyone that their best interest was to put their trust and this ultimate power in your hands? I would. I think anyone who was honest with themselves would say the same.

- Broadcaster Anchore, released September 27, 970 Y.A.

The weeks passed, then the months. All the while, like

clockwork, Moar Schitte showed up at the library for his biweekly sessions and asked his questions. Each time that he came, Davina made sure to be at the front desk to greet him, and every time after he left, Puren made sure to voice his disapproval. Sully wondered if she should say something to her assistants, but she didn't in the end. As long as their work didn't suffer, their personal life was no business of hers.

Then, one day at the end of a session in the early winter when the snow laid thick on her library steps, Moar said, "I think this is going to be our last interview."

"Oh? Do you have everything you need for your thesis?" Sully couldn't help but be surprised and a little disappointed. She had gotten used to him and his endless questions. Though she would never complain about her work, his presence was a welcome break from the stacks.

"Definitely—more than enough." Moar smiled. "You've been so helpful. You've given me an in-depth view of the innards of the library system and the role of a librarian. I couldn't have put together my main argument and backed it up without our sessions."

"Will I get a preview?"

"I want it to be a surprise. I'm working on the final draft now. I'll submit it to my committee soon and defend it this spring. I can send you a copy once it's approved."

"I would like that." Looking at his easy smile and easier demeanor, Sully knew that she would miss him. Even though every last word, expression, and article of clothing from their sessions was imprinted in her memory, it was not the same thing as his presence. "I might even add it to the stacks."

"*Really?* Maybe, you should read it first," he winked.

"I'm sure it will be great."

"It won't be disappointing, that's for sure."

They stood at the same time, and Sully walked around her desk to open the door for him. She held out a hand for him to shake. "It's been a good time, and I hope you'll stop by the library as an actual patron after you've graduated."

He ignored the hand and reached out to envelope her in a bear hug. "Don't be a stranger," he said. Then, he released her and walked out. As the door closed slowly after him, Sully wondered if this was the last time she would see Moar Schitte.

"It's out!" Davina came into Sully's office with a face full of smiles.

Sully looked up from the page she was working on. The full volume, titled *Against the Odds: Hard Lessons Learned from the Remmington Conflict,* was a replacement for its predecessor, one of several deteriorating volumes pulled last month from the *Military History* aisle. Sully had been meaning to get to the thick pile for several weeks now and was happy to finally be able to block off a chunk of time to work on transcribing their replacements. "Moar's thesis?" she asked.

"Yup! I requested a copy from LCU and just got it in the mail. Here it is." Davina plopped a sheath of paper onto Sully's desk.

"Have you read it?"

"No, I thought you should be the first one since his thesis is based on your interviews. I call dibs afterwards though. I wonder if he mentioned me?"

"Thank you, Davina. I'll read through it after I get through this stack." Sully nodded toward the volumes in the corner. Tempting as it was to let Moar's work distract her from her responsibilities, she had neglected these books for long enough.

"Alright, happy reading." Davina turned and walked toward the door. Before walking through, she paused and turned around again. "I wanted to ask you if I could have next Saturday off."

"Oh? Is there a special occasion?" Sully was a bit surprised. In the two and a half years since Davina had begun working at the library, Sully could count on one hand the number of times she had requested leave.

"A friend of mine is graduating, and I want to be at his graduation party. It's not the biggest deal, but I figured he's only going to graduate once. I might as well be there to support him if I can."

Graduation? Davina had been out of school for several years, and Sully doubted that she had any close friends her age who had yet to complete their studies. "Is it Moar's?" She raised an eyebrow.

"Okay . . . fine, it's his graduation. I swear I didn't ask or anything. This invitation card slipped out when I picked up his paper. It was addressed to me." Davina held up a white card-stock sheet with a single black matriculation cap printed on it. *Davina, it would be amazing to have you at my graduation party next Saturday at 13:00 hour at the LCU campus's Comstock Hall -Moar.* The flowing handwritten script fit perfectly in the limited space at the bottom of the card.

"Why didn't he just come to the library and ask you in person?" Sully asked. "It would have been good to see him and catch up."

Davina shrugged. "Yeah, he has been weirdly shy since you two finished the interviews. Maybe he was just too busy to stop by and say hi."

"Well, if Puren can fill in for you that day, then I don't have a problem with it."

"Yay! I'm sure he'll say yes! Thanks Sully!" Davina turned and skipped through the door.

Shaking her head ruefully, Sully said, "Poor Puren."

Sully would not be adding Moar's thesis to her precious Library. Not now, not ever.

From the first word to the last, his thesis was an excoriation of the Republic's library system. He questioned the founders' wisdom in preserving the People's memory within their hallowed halls. He denied her and her peers' credibility by mocking the infallible nature of their eidetic memories. And he backed up his arguments by twisting each word from their interviews. Where Sully had been proud, Moar created arrogance. Where Sully had been certain, Moar produced indifference. Where Sully had been prudent, Moar fabricated recklessness. He made it seem as if librarians were inimical actors manipulating the

People's memories. He made it seem obvious. Only a gullible fool would believe that librarians held the People's best interests.

He was no friend to the library. He had never been.

This was the first time that Sully thought her photographic memory was a curse. She wished that she could scrub the contents of Moar's thesis from her mind and pull out every last spiteful word that had dug its tenacious claws into her brain. She should have stopped reading at the first paragraph, but her sheer disbelief kept her hooked on the page to the very end.

I won't disappoint.

My thesis will stand out.

Waste this face on the stacks?

Nothing much but change the world.

The worst thing was that he hadn't lied to her. Not in the truest sense of the word. He told her just enough so that she would fill in the blanks with her own assumptions. She thought that he had the same appreciation for the library as she did. With the ambition that she had glimpsed, he could have gone far and reached the public with that same appreciation. How could Sully have gotten it so wrong? She felt sick.

Her only consolation was the knowledge that theses rarely left the halls of the university. The average person in the Republic read three books a year. She doubted that they would touch the work of some no-name student.

Moar's thesis would die in obscurity with Sully the only one to remember it.

My argument is a simple one. We have been taught since birth that librarians hold our best interests in mind. That they are the only ones qualified to preserve history. You may ask them why, and their response is that it has always been this way.

Dear listeners, I want you all to ask yourselves why. Furthermore, ask yourselves why it should be this way?

If you think about it, the answer is easy. It shouldn't be.

No one should control your history but yourself.

- Broadcaster Anchore, released January 21, 971 Y.A.

As the months passed, Sully's work continued in a blur of endless library tasks, and Moar's thesis—not quite forgotten—was pushed to the back of her mind. January was focused on the intake and categorization of new volumes sent by the Recordkeepers in the Capital. She and her assistants painstakingly poured over each text, committing every letter, paragraph break, and punctuation mark to memory before adding it to their existing collection, sorted first by topic, then year and author.

February was focused on inventorying the texts that needed repair, and Sully sent Puren grousing into the stacks to note down any text that showed signs of wear in the library's record book. Davina showed up late near the end of the task and seemed to receive both Sully's reprimand and Puren's complaining with indifference. Sully was surprised by her assistant's new attitude, but she had never had an issue with her performance in the past and assumed that this sudden apathy was fleeting. It helped that Puren's inspection only noted down eight volumes that needed repair and not complete replacement, a featherlight workload for the next few months.

March was filled with that repair. Davina was rarely seen, and Sully, with her nose buried in *The Fall of Despotism and the Rise of Amnesty: Volumes I – VIII*, hardly noticed.

April was uncharacteristically slow. The month was the penultimate before university finals, and the library—typically filled to the brim with students bent over their course books in panicked, last-minute studying—was quiet. Sully and Puren used the time to cross off many of the administrative tasks left on his assistantship checklist. She wanted to do the same for Davina, but lately it seemed as if she had only one assistant.

The resignation letter that came at the end of the month was no surprise to anyone. Sully only wished that it offered more of an explanation.

May was full of confrontations. It started with Puren showing up in her office library with a radio. He was clearly agitated as he set the radio on Sully's desk with a quiet *thump*, plugged in the cord, raised the antennae, and turned the knob, stopping when the small screen read, *93.4*. "Listen," he said.

I propose that this was a mistake. Librarians are just as human and fallible as the rest of us . . .

Sully recognized that voice instantly—"It's Moar"—and listened with growing unease as her old interviewer voiced aloud the same arguments that he had made in his thesis with a soft but undeniable fervor.

"That fucker."

It was instinctual to admonish Puren even though Sully felt the same. "So, this is what he ended up doing after graduation," she said after they had finished listening to the entire broadcast.

"It's not right," Puren said, "He's been calling himself Broadcaster Anchore. Somehow, he got access to a station. I don't listen to the radio, but my mom told me about it when I was home on Sunday. She said that he's been broadcasting this shit for months and has built up a following. Who in their right mind would follow that turd?"

"Thank you for bringing this to my attention." Sully stood and walked around her desk to the cord in the wall. She unplugged it and coiled the cord around her hand. Lowering the antennae, she lifted the radio and held it out to Puren.

He didn't take it. "How are you so calm about this? He's telling people that librarians are the enemy! And they *believe* him."

"I'm just as angry as you, but this is only a distraction. We have a job to do. If you feel like you can't focus today, then take the rest of the day off. Give the radio back to your mom. Moar's words are just that, words. Forget about them." Sully knew what a futile thing it was to tell someone with an eidetic memory to forget, but she hoped that Puren would at least ignore Moar Schitte as she resolutely did.

"You need to take this more seriously. You should start your own broadcast. Tell the People he's lying to them!"

Sully shook her head. "I'm no broadcaster."

"Then bring this to the Librarian Consortium. One of you needs to speak out against him. He's not going away, and people are starting to listen to him. Look what happened with Davina."

"Davina left because this library was not a good fit for her."

"You can't seriously believe that." Puren's tone was as biting as a fresh papercut. "She left because she was listening to him. She believes what he's saying. And she's not the only one!"

"A librarian's role is in the library. Not some recording studio. You'll understand this when you become head of this institution."

"Fine, even if you think Davina leaving was just some coincidence. How can you ignore what else is happening? April was so slow. No one has walked through our doors in weeks! We're losing patrons. If he keeps going, we'll lose the People's trust."

Sully shook her head. "Puren, you have only worked here for six years. I have been here for most of my life, so believe me when I say that trust is not so easily eroded. This Library has existed since the founding of our Republic, and for that entire time, the People have trusted in our ability to guard their history and memory. That will not be changed by one dissenting voice. Go home and come back tomorrow with a fresh mindset."

She could tell that Puren wanted to keep arguing, but he only shook his head and, taking the radio from her hands, said, "You know best, Librarian Smith."

Enough is enough.

    - Broadcaster Anchore, released June 13, 971 Y.A.

It was a blistering hot summer day when Touchstone Library received its last visitor. The man was well known to the library and its librarian. Young with brown eyes, long lashes, and white straight teeth. He was tanner than when Sully had seen him last in the middle of winter, three years ago, but he still had that same prominent brow and curly, black hair.

It was Puren's day off, one of two days that had once been occupied by Davina, and Sully was alone at the front desk. "You have some nerve coming here," was her only greeting to the visitor.

"Hello Sully," Moar Schitte said.

Similar to the first day that Moar had shown up at her library, it had been a slow day—her library patrons, once a steady stream, had trickled dry weeks ago—but unlike then, Sully had much less patience for her visitor now. "Only my friends call me Sully. What do you want?" she bit out.

"I'm not here to fight. I only came as a courtesy to Davina. I've been very successful as Broadcaster Anchore and have built up quite a following. People across the Republic are calling for the end of the library system. I'm not sure what this will mean for librarians, but I imagine it won't be good." He delivered it all in a bland tone as if he was ordering coffee on a Sunday afternoon. It made it seem as if Sully, in her shock and outrage, was the unreasonable one.

"You can't be serious."

"I'm afraid so. Pack your bags and leave with your head held high. It will be much more dignified than being forcibly removed." Moar held out his hand for Sully to shake. "Despite everything, I hope you know that it wasn't personal. I have the deepest respect for you and this library."

Sully ignored his hand. He was lucky she didn't spit in it.

"How could you do this then? You owe me a better

explanation than that."

He dropped his hand. "Do you know that you were the fourth librarian I approached? The other librarians I asked didn't give me the time of day as soon as they learned what my family name was. It didn't matter that I was a student struggling to make something new for myself beyond the name I was given at birth. It didn't matter that I was genuinely curious about the library system. They all had their convenient excuses to politely say no. But you, a Smith serving as a Biblios librarian, were the only one willing to talk to a Schitte."

"This again? Family names are a thing of the past."

"*Hah!*" Moar's laugh was scornful. "You really believe that? What a privilege it must be to be a librarian, wrapped in your books and isolated from the outside world. You, with your photographic memory, may have been the exception to the rule, but the rest of the world still cares immensely about a person's family name. You asked 'how could I do this?' Easy, it was the quickest path to *be* someone. What were interviews and one thesis going to do when it came to applying for political advisor jobs? All they did was take one look at my surname and pass over my application. The only way I could get their attention was to create my own base. I couldn't do that by saying the same things that have been said over and over."

"*The People's identity lies in their memory. Their memory is stored in the library. And the Library's guardian is its Librarian.* You're the one who gave me the answer on that first day. I had to shock people. I had to play with their outrage. What happens when the institution that everyone has always believed in ends up working against their interests? Manipulating them? That's a betrayal that will shake anyone's trust to its core. And here I was, the convenient messenger, ready to fill the vacuum."

"You're wrong. Libraries were part of the founding of this Republic. You won't break the People's trust in us so easily."

Moar shook his head, sadly. "That's the problem with you librarians. You can't be bothered by what's going on in the outside world unless it's mentioned in one of your precious books. I'm not breaking the People's trust in you. I've already *broken* it. People are furious. You're a study of history. You know better than most what people are capable of when they're angry. I won't say it again. Leave before it's too late." Moar turned and with a parting, "Good-bye Librarian Smith," left the library.

It seemed as if Moar had taken all the sound with him, and the library was dead silent in his absence. It didn't help that Sully, the lone inhabitant, was quiet. The library was waiting for her decision.

She got up slowly, turned in a circle to take in the floor to ceiling shelves that had been both her metropolis and her sanctuary. She walked slowly to the back of the library and unlocked the door to her suite. She packed a small suitcase filled with only the necessities, and as she walked back through the stacks, she ran her fingers across the tomes one final time. She knew each and every one of them intimately. They had spilled their inner secrets to her, trusted her with their testimonies like the greatest of confidantes.

That was the worst part of it. Sully felt as if she was betraying them by leaving them now, but what choice did she have?

Moar was many things, but he had never lied to her.

Sully opened the doors to the outside and locked them behind her. She looked at the towering stone façade one last time. "I won't forget," she promised the library that had been her home for over thirty years.

After leaving the library, Sully had gone to the only other place she knew. Her assistant had met her at the front door of his home. Wordlessly, he had let her inside, and wordlessly, he had listened as she had recounted what Moar had said. *You were right*, she had finished. *I'm sorry.*

Puren had shaken his head firmly and engulfed her in a hug. It had been warm and comforting in the exact way that she had desperately needed. Had she really once thought that he was not good with people? In his arms, Sully had cried.

It had been weeks since then. She now inhabited Puren's spare bedroom, though it would have been more accurate to say that she inhabited his spare bed. Outside of getting up to use the bathroom and eat, she rarely left the bed. Maybe it was mourning; maybe it was despair. Whatever the reason, Sully didn't feel like doing anything.

Then, one day, Puren came into her bedroom with a radio. He set it on her bedside table, plugged it in, and turned the knob until the screen read *93.4*. "Listen," was all he said before leaving the room.

Moar Schitte's voice filled the space, and Sully listened as he crowed his victory over the library system. She listened as he celebrated how the People had stormed into libraries across the Republic and gutted them of the precious texts she had spent a lifetime preserving. She listened with her fists clenched under the blankets as he glorified a bonfire that could be seen from the heavens.

We are finally free of libraries and their librarians. Let us write our own history now.

Sully got out of bed.

What did Sulivena Smith know about defending her country with guns and steel? She was no soldier. What did she know of marching in the streets? She was no protester. What did she know of reaching thousands over the air with a message enticing in its simplicity? She was no broadcaster like Anchore.

All Sully knew was her library and her books. All she had was her memory. So, she used it. Day after day, hiding in Puren's spare bedroom, Sully wrote in the blank notebooks that her assistant supplied.

Moar Schitte was changing things. Sully could see it clearly in the dissonance of her memories. Where once there was only a single version of fact, she now saw two versions, the original one that she recalled from memory and another—an insidious stranger—superimposed over the original. It was a jarring feeling to have two versions of history exist in her mind at the same time, and if it had not been for Puren, she would have thought she was going mad.

Schitte and his ilk thought that they could so easily change the People's memory. They believed that they had rewritten the Republic's history with the replacement of her beloved texts by his revisionist history. But they were wrong. There was one last copy, stored in a librarian's memory, and as long as she lived, she was determined that it would never be forgotten.

So, Sully wrote. Fueled by the stale bread, salted meat, and root vegetables that Puren forced her to eat, she wrote. She filled notebook upon notebook with words that she recalled from her eidetic memory. She steadfastly ignored that second, false memory, and not a single word from it graced the pages of these notebooks. It was lonely work, and it was exhausting. There was pain in her hands and an even greater pain in her breast.

Still, she wrote.

My name is Sulivena Smith, and I am the Librarian of what once was Touchstone Library. As far as I know, I may be the last Librarian, so I write this from my memory as one final testimony to the People's history. Within these texts, you'll find a version of history, diligently recorded since the founding of our Republic in the Year of Amnesty 466. It will be different from what you know and have been told, but I assure you that it is the truth, a direct transcription from a librarian's memory.

I know that you won't believe me. There was a time when the refrain of a librarian's memory was all that was needed to convince you of the accuracy and veracity of a text. That time was when institutions across the Republic stood steadfast against the vagaries of human nature. That time was before Moar Schitte or, as you know him, Broadcaster Anchore convinced you otherwise.

I know that time is past, and I am not bitter. I mourn the loss of our libraries. More than that, I mourn the loss of your confidence in our guardianship, but in transcribing these texts once more, I have had my moment of insight. Curious, isn't it, how recalling the past can bring such clarity to the present?

Though it pains me to say, Broadcaster Anchore was not entirely wrong. We are librarians, and though our memories are infallible, we are not. Our founders were wrong to place the sole guardianship of your history in our hands. Neither should your history be the honeyed words of Anchore. Your history is yours, and yours alone.

So, I ask you to do this one thing for the last Librarian.

Read these texts.

And remember.

-From the first passage of *The Librarian's Memory*, written 974 Y.A., recovered and digitized May 29, 1078 Y.A.

THE KNOCKER

C.H. SCOTT

My new line cook walked straight to their prep station and julienned carrots as if in their home kitchen. But this was *my* kitchen, where fish don't do shit without checking with the old timers first. I may run this place like a three-star restaurant, but it's still a prison mess. If the lack of social graces wasn't enough to tell me I was dealing with a knocker, the lack of hair, the porcelain skin, and the black olive eyes sealed it. I didn't request a synthetic. In two weeks, after I served them a fine dinner, the parole board would consider my case. That meal—and my behavior up to that point—must be perfect. Warden Xiang knew how I felt about machines replacing chefs. He was screwing with me.

My other line cook, Reza, chopped onions and watched the scene with the eager grin of a hungry tiger. I glared and he sliced his thumb, cursing as he brought it to his mouth. My sous,

Johnny Brass, smirked, the tip of his battered chef's knife resting on the dimple of his clean-shaven chin. Watching how it would play out, ready to take over. These guys didn't give a damn who I was before arriving at Sisyphus MinSec Corrections. The media empire, the Michelin stars. None of it. On the inside, clout reset to zero each day. You marked your territory each hour.

I reached for my old standby, sarcasm, and called out across the canteen. "Bonjour Miss Childs, is there anything I can get for you?"

Reza and Johnny snickered but the knocker ignored me, batonneting potatoes at a million miles per hour. The technique was solid, but a knocker lacks the art to being a chef. Literally no sense of taste.

I moved on to good, old-fashioned prison bullying. "Hey knocker, I'm talking to you!"

The android looked at me with the vacant gaze that all knockers have. "I think I have everything I need, thank you." It went back to work.

My blood boiled as the chance of a clean parole hearing ebbed away. "You do know who I am?"

The android turned and squinted for a split second, taking me in. Squinted? That was different. "Yes, you're Otto Bane. Formerly *chef de cuisine* of the Michelin-starred Osteria Otto in Shanghai, as well as numerous other high-end restaurants. Formerly the celebrity chef of the long-running and highly rated culinary series, *Bane on the Beat*. Father to Zara Bane, author of the tell-all book . . ."

"Don't fucking talk about my daughter."

The knocker paused like it was processing this. "But you're her father." It searched my eyes for a second, then continued: "You're currently serving ten years for evading local and planetary taxes."

"Allegedly!"

"Also accused of poisoning the ambassador from the Kalaallit Nunaat delegation."

"I didn't know they were allergic to purslane!"

"Allegedly."

Johnny snickered and Reza whistled, glad to hear me taking some heat. I hammered the controls on the nearest comm: "Please ask Warden Xiang to visit the galley. We have a problem."

The knocker, annoyingly, went back to dicing shallots.

Xiang Jin was the assistant warden and roundly feared by inmates and staff alike. Former Snow Leopard commando and seemingly pissed off that he was dispatched to a minimum-security joint like Sisyphus—full of sheepish tax evaders, ethically unmoored geneticists, and market manipulators—where he couldn't break necks with impunity. Xiang glided in like a cat, wearing a hand-stitched suit that was way above his pay grade, two guards trailing behind. Not that he needed them. He towered over me, the guards, everyone. This wasn't an augmentation; he was just an enormous guy.

I cleared my throat and tried to strike a balance between "Please don't kill me," for Xiang and "I'm not afraid of you," for the staff. "Warden, respectfully, I didn't ask for an android. Please take it away."

Xiang shot a split-second look at the knocker, then back to me. "It's not an appliance for your kitchen, Bane. You think we'd spend android money on you? Or on feeding your lot? Prison labor's still cheaper."

"What's its designation? It's not part of the DHS line, is it?" Domestic Help Synthetics are junk. Nothing worse than consumer grade tech in your kitchen.

"Němec's not part of any line. It's an inmate."

"Excuse me? It has a name?"

Xiang smacked my head as a warning, which left my ears ringing. "You reached your question limit, Bane. Get back to work." He bellowed across the kitchen: "Chow's in half an hour!" With that he turned and left, the guards trailing behind like baby ducks following their mama.

A commercial android flat-out refuses to do anything illegal. Even the military ones follow international humanitarian code. If any of them break the law or are backdoored, they get zeroed-out or scrapped. There's not even a reliable way to figure out what went wrong. It didn't make sense for Němec to be an inmate.

I took in the totality of the knocker's station, where it had set up a perfect *mise en place* for the night's menu. Every ingredient uniformly chopped and in the proper bin for maximum speed and minimum reach. The stainless-steel work surface clean and shiny, knives out of the way and hanging like icicles. Exactly like my books and streams instruct. Němec stood at attention and bored into me with those olive eyes.

I worked with a lot of junkies, flakes, and dilettantes over the years—and that's just in the restaurant business. Prison life is a consommé of the outside world, reduced and clarified to its purest form. Everyone has an agenda, something they want, a way of ingratiating themselves. This smelled of Němec playing me. But what the hell would an android want?

Johnny and Reza leaned over their stations, grinning like a couple of younger brothers who just saw their parent chew out the eldest for something they themselves did.

"Glad I could make your day, gentlemen," I said. "Reza: get your head out of your ass and your rolls out of the oven. They're burning. Johnny: get your chowder in the tureen before it cools. It'll curdle if reheated."

"Yes, Chef," in unison. My favorite sound.

Our fellow inmates lumbered into the mess ahead of schedule, noisily pulling up benches and barking insults at each other. Soon they'd be hungry and restless. Xiang was right: dinner must be served. I've never been late for a seating. And I would be damned before I'd let the knocker make this the first.

From then on, my gaze hovered over the knocker like one of Sisyphus' security drones. At lunch the next day, the android flicked its wrist over a steaming pot of mushroom soup, as if sprinkling pepper or salt, but nothing was visible. I'd chalk it up to an affectation, but knockers don't have flair.

I stormed over to Němec's station just as it was about to add some more of whatever it was, grabbed its wrist and twisted. "What the hell did you put in that soup?" I growled.

Its face was an empty plate. "Ingredients."

My jaw hardened. I'm used to my crew at least having some fear of me. After all, I controlled their continued employment in this cushy gig.

"Okay, I see," I said. "You want to make a visit to Warden Xiang? Maybe get on another detail?"

"No, I'm perfectly suited for the kitchen. It was one of my many roles at home."

"You're not perfectly suited for *my* kitchen. In my kitchen, I need obedience."

"You don't trust me, Chef?"

"I don't."

"Because I'm artificial."

"Because you're a prison inmate! You obviously fucked up before."

The squint again. I must've hit home.

"Get Xiang in here," I yelled over my shoulder to Johnny. I held tight to the knocker's wrist so it couldn't get rid of the evidence.

When Xiang finally arrived, he didn't say a word, just arched an eyebrow.

Screw looking tough for my men, I resorted to pleading. "Warden, please remove this machine from my kitchen. It put something in the soup, then refused my order to tell me what it was."

Xiang folded his pythonic forearms across his chest. "Let's see the hand, Němec."

Němec released its palm, which of course was completely

empty. Xiang's fingers whipped to the back of my neck, his thumb and forefinger digging into pressure points below my ears.

"You can't serve that soup," I sputtered.

"Oh, now you're ordering *me*, Bane?" Xiang's fingers were like drill bits. "You and Němec are coming with me." He turned to Johnny, who stood at attention, and wiped the smirk off his face. "Brass, make sure this meal gets served."

Solitary on Sisyphus is not so much a hole as a basketball court, mostly because it is, in fact, an unused basketball court fitted with a single bunk, shower, and toilet. While you'd think this would be better than a confined area, the vast, empty space only made you feel lonelier.

With nowhere to sit except the bunk, Němec and I sat awkwardly, side-by-side, in the cavernous room while we waited on Xiang to investigate my accusations. Two security drones whirred above us like pale, metal dragonflies. The knocker ignored me and watched the drones with its dark, insectoid eyes. Machine or not, I know when someone's annoyed with me.

I decided to appeal to the android's sense of reason. "Look," I said. "My parole hearing is in less than two weeks. I don't know what you're trying to pull, but I can't have you mucking up my chance of getting out of here."

Nothing but silence. It rubbed its forefinger and thumb together in a slow rhythm. A nervous habit? Then: "What keeps you going, Chef?"

I shrugged. "What do you think? I like to cook. Create new culinary experiences. Run a kitchen."

"That's obvious." Němec shifted his thousand-yard stare across the court, looking beyond its walls. "What I mean is: what's waiting for you on the outside?"

Zara's face hit me first. That sticky grin the first time I made her homemade ice cream when she was six years old: Rocky Road with my own masala twist. All the reviews, awards, and venture capital up to that point couldn't equal the feeling I got watching her believe I worked magic.

Fuck it. She was eighteen now and made it clear at the trial two years ago that she didn't want anything to do with me. Even more clear when she wrote that book.

I forced a cold smile and wistful air, which wasn't too hard because I'd dreamed of this before. "I still have an agent. Investors. Production companies that want to work with me again. A whole new concept built around my reform." A classic redemption story. The vulnerable side of Otto Bane. My way. My agent would be at Sisyphus in a couple days to discuss this very thing.

Němec grunted. Or at least that's what it sounded like.

"Okay then," I grumbled. "How about you? What's waiting for you out there?"

The double doors opened, cutting off the knocker's reply. Xiang and a fish I'd noticed once or twice from the mess entered. The newcomer's oily skin and disheveled, steel-wool hair contrasted with Xiang's precision grooming like a biocosmetic engineer's before-and-after dream. His shoestring-fry physique spoke of someone who considered himself too busy to eat, which meant I disliked him immediately.

"You have five minutes, Němec," punctuating it with a dagger-like forefinger to the newcomer's sternum. Another Němec?

The new Němec smiled and placed his hand on the android's shoulder, as if greeting an old friend.

"Why are you here?" The knocker asked, his question a frigid wall.

"They thought I could talk to you," the man said, his accent possibly Eastern European. "Make you more . . . compliant?"

"You won't."

"That's what I told them."

"Besides, there's nothing to talk about. *I* did nothing wrong. I'm here because of you."

"That's what I told them as well. They put you in here, anyway."

"He who sows the wind reaps the storm, Doctor."

The new Němec grimaced. I shifted on the bed like a co-worker at a holiday party sitting next to combative spouses.

Finally, the new Němec asked, "Have you spoken with Aroha?"

"Not since they came for me," the knocker said. "They're afraid I'll hack the communications system by whistling into it or something."

"Would you like me to get a message to her?"

The knocker paused and regarded the security drones, their cameras trained on us. "Tell her it's time we see each other again," it said. A shadow of a smile played on the android's lips. Or did it?

"Of course!" The new Němec beamed, clapping the knocker on the shoulder. "It was good working with you, Tomáš. I'd like to do it again. Even in here."

Tomáš? How many names did this knocker have?

"If I have any say whatsoever," the knocker said, "I'll make sure that never happens."

The new Němec raised an eyebrow but only shrugged. He turned and left, one of the drones following.

"What the hell was that all about?" I asked. "Who was that guy?"

"Dr. Rene Němec," Němec said. "My creator. The reason I'm here."

"Your creator? What the hell did you two do to end up in here?"

Němec said nothing.

"Okay," I said, "who's this Aroha?"

"Aroha's the reason I'm getting out," the knocker replied.

The doors swished and Xiang charged in like a tiger. I stood and he shoved me back into my seat. He looked at Němec and arced his thumb towards the door. "Back to your cell," he said, motioning for the remaining drone to follow. This made me nervous. Alone with Xiang without cameras is not a place you want to be.

He launched into me. "We checked the recordings from the kitchen cameras. He didn't put anything in the soup. No more of this prima donna shit. You're both going back to the kitchen."

I figured this would happen, but I know what I saw. "That machine's up to something," I said.

Xiang ran a hand over his crewcut and puffed his cheeks, looking more resigned than upset. "I wish he wasn't here either, Bane, but you're hoping to quench your thirst by thinking of plums. You have it easy: I'm the one with my face plastered all over the news. You think that housing the first sentient android is a picnic?"

"Wait a minute . . . sentient? That's illegal."

Xiang looked at me like I'm an idiot. "Why do you think both Němecs are here?"

That explained it. Intersystem law dictates that androids can't be self-aware. The populace demands it. Self-preservation. "When do they get out?"

"Ten years for the engineer, if he behaves, which I don't think will be a problem. He's stiff as an old board. The android . . . ?" Xiang shrugged his massive shoulders.

I'm not always an idiot. "The knocker's not getting out, is it?"

"Let's just say its rights are in legal limbo. That it's sentient is about the only thing the courts agree on. Does it matter? Synthetics don't experience time the way you and I do, Bane. Besides, what does it have to go back to?"

You know when you flambé crêpes Suzette and the fire leaps out of the pan? You know it's coming, but you're still a little surprised. That's the way this next idea came out of my mouth. "If I can help you get rid of this knocker . . . ."

"Bane . . . ."

"Not like that. I mean sent to a max or something. If I can do that, would you back me up at the parole board next month?"

Xiang sucked his cheeks, considering. "We'll see how things develop."

That was good enough for me.

The next day we wrapped up dinner and the crew filed out. It was about to get as quiet as the mess got.

"Hey, Němec," I called, "can I hold you back?"

The knocker stopped and looked at me, then went back to its *mise*. I walked up to it and whispered, "Not here. Let's go to the freezer."

The freezer was large enough for months, if not years, worth of food. Its cavernous expanse was so filled with boxes and cans that Němec and I had to stand a breath's distance from each other. Soon it would be arctic-cold in there.

"Look, I'm sorry we got off to a bad start," I began, trying to sound sensible, "but I've been thinking about what you said. About what keeps me going."

Němec's face didn't give anything away. "What do you want, Chef?"

"A deal. I know you have something brewing."

"Why do you say that?"

"Because you're smarter than me and even I know they're not letting you out of here. If you have something on the outside, you can't let that go."

I think Němec smiled, which was as awkward as a bird walking: it could do it, but you could tell that wasn't its natural state. "And what do you want in return?"

I knew what the android wanted to hear. "Contact my daughter. Tell her I miss her and want to see her. She doesn't accept my comms."

Němec studied me. If it contacted Zara, I was sure she'd say no. Not that it mattered. The knocker wasn't going home.

"I'll do this."

"Good. Where do we start?"

At lunch Němec sprinkled something into the roux, but this time I knew it was coming. I wasn't told what it was—just part of the knocker's plan—but it must be nanoscale if it wasn't detectable. I didn't really care; that's something Xiang could sort out later. If all went well, the knocker would be out of here and out of my hair by that afternoon.

After lunch, with the knocker gone back to its bunk, I pinged Xiang on the comm.

"Němec's going to make a move this afternoon," I whispered. "He's trying to get out of here."

"Nobody can get out of here," Xiang said.

"He has a plan. I don't know the details, but I think he can pull it off."

"I need more than just your hunch. He has a visitor this afternoon and they're expecting to see him. Speaking of which, your agent's also on the list."

"That's fine. It'll take some time. I'll let you know when I'm done on my end. Just be ready." I cut the comms, feeling a little smug ordering Xiang around.

"Was that Warden Xiang?" Němec said behind me. I didn't hear him come in. My heart pounded but I tried to remain calm.

"Yeah, he just wanted some changes to the menu." Then, just to see what Němec would do. "Also, something about visitors." If bringing visitors up surprised the knocker, it didn't show it.

"That's why I came back. Come with me to the Family Visiting Unit."

The knocker rubbed its forefinger again in that nervous way, but otherwise its face was blank. Was this a trick to keep me close? Did it know?

"Why?"

"There's someone I want you to meet."

The FVU buzzed with families. Partners nuzzled on the plush couches. Kids screamed at and taunted each other across raucous hologame tables. None of my crew were there, which suited me fine.

A woman stood when Němec and I entered. Tall, brown skin. Wearing a tweed business suit and horn-rimmed glasses. Probably in her forties but could've been from the last century. I can't remember the last time I saw anyone wearing glasses.

"Good to see you, Tomáš," she said, smiling. A first name basis, just like the doctor, his creator.

"You as well, Aroha," Němec said, simply. It couldn't take his eyes off her and seemed to be at a loss for words.

"You're its lawyer?" I asked, since Němec was tongue-tied.

"More of an advocate," she corrected, "and more of a philosopher and ethicist. Dr. Aroha Vainerere." She extended a hand, which I shook. It was warm and firm, with no hint of nervousness.

Němec took her hands and cupped them in his, holding them against his chest. She didn't seem concerned or surprised, merely smiled. "Dr. Vainerere worked with Dr. Němec," the knocker explained, quickly. "Aroha, this is Otto Bane. He's helping me."

The doctor arched an eyebrow at me. "Indeed. I remember your conviction, Mr. Bane. Even in *Bane on the Beat* you weren't exactly known for your good deeds."

"It made for good entertainment. That's not me." Of course it was me.

"We have to help him, Aroha," the knocker interjected. "When does your loopcar leave?"

"In an hour."

"I only have a few minutes." Němec was speaking quickly, almost panicky, its forearms quivering as it did so.

Something was off, beyond me feeling like a third wheel, but I couldn't put my finger on it. Thankfully, my agent arrived and sat down at one of the desks. I caught her eye and nodded.

"My agent's here," I said. "I'll catch you later, Němec. Good meeting you, Doctor."

Aroha smiled as I left. Němec said nothing and didn't take

his eyes off her.

My agent wore a slim, turquoise kimono and a tall hat that looked like a giant cheese grater. It was a testament to how beautiful she was that she made even that look good, though I'd never let her know it. "Hey Felicia," I said, sitting across from her, "did they search that hat for hacksaws and pickaxes?"

Felicia smiled; her teeth sculpted Chiclets of perfection. "I told them there was no need," she said. "I can be very persuasive."

"That's what I pay you for."

Felicia launched into a rundown of interest for a reality stream based on my comeback. We already knew the comeback was inevitable. The investors had lined up. The São Paulo location chosen months ago. It was all a matter of telling a good story. I nodded as Felicia spoke, though I couldn't help but turn around every minute or two and sneak a glance at the knocker chatting away with Aroha. I'd never seen him so animated.

"Are you listening, Otto?" Felicia asked.

"Uh, yeah," I said.

"No, you're not." Felicia looked behind me. "Is that the famous android?"

"Unfortunately, yes."

She stared at the pair for a minute. "It looks like he's in love."

"Impossible," I mumbled. "A knocker can't love."

"Otto, your crusty heart may have forgotten what infatuation looks like. But I get that look at least once a week. It's in love."

Němec pressed Aroha's hands to his lips, then his forehead,

gently. I felt my breath catch and skin go prickly, like when you see the same, familiar sunset that you've seen a million times in a new way. I felt it when I met my wife. I felt it when I first laid eyes on my newborn daughter.

Felicia was right. The fucker *was* in love.

After we left the FVU, Němec went back to its bunk. I went where I always did when my life suddenly took a strange turn: to my kitchen. I needed to think. I needed to breathe.

My brain wasn't going to let me make anything complicated, so I settled on my ultimate comfort food. I whipped a couple eggs with milk, sprinkled in some five-spice, let two slices of day-old brioche soak in it, and threw them on a buttered skillet for my signature French toast. As it sizzled, that nutty, caramelized smell of the Maillard reaction hit my nostrils and soothed me.

When it was golden-brown I threw it on a plate, sprinkled on some powdered sugar, and took my first bite. I saw Zara's three-year-old face light up with awe after I made her French toast for the first time back in our Singapore condo. She looked at me like I'd just performed magic. It became the go-to meal anytime she had a bad scrape, a rough day at school, or one of her fish died.

I made it the day after her mom passed away, when she was only twelve. That same day I called Felicia and told her I was interested in a three-cookbook deal and a stream. After that, I threw myself into my work and was no longer there for Zara's bad scrapes. The start of the four-year spiral that led me to do *anything* to keep my little cooking empire going. That led me to Sisyphus. That led my daughter away from me.

The knocker had someone on the outside, I'd closed mine off and this place made it even worse. Was I jealous? Hell yes, I was. Did I think he deserved his shot on the outside? Sure. I dropped my fork, went over to the comm, and punched up Xiang. "Warden, I have something to tell you. Němec . . . ."

My voice choked and I couldn't utter a word. In my peripheral vision I saw a pale hand turn off the comm. Němec, his voice even, said, "Follow me, Chef."

I did, but not because I wanted to. There was no struggle or jerkiness like you see in old B-movies of someone manipulated by a telekinetic. I walked, like you do, but it wasn't me doing the walking. Němec led me into the freezer and shut the door behind us. The cold quickly seeped into my body. We stood close, my breath materializing into a puff of fog. Of course, nothing came out of Němec's mouth. He didn't breathe. He didn't feel the cold at all. A different kind of chill seeped into my heart. This might be it. Forget parole boards, time off for good behavior, and any other delusion I had that gave me hope I'd have a restaurant again. See my daughter again. Despite the cold, my heart boiled in my chest.

Němec looked at me with a pained expression. "Why?"

Something released and I found my voice. There was nothing to say but the truth. "My parole hearing," I said, my mouth dry. "I thought if I gave you up, it would increase my odds of getting out of here. But I changed my mind. I was going to tell

Xiang it was a mistake."

Němec looked skeptical.

I added, "You love her, don't you? Aroha."

A pause. "I think so."

"I saw you. You do."

Němec studied me for a minute, then relaxed and I felt the grip on me slacken a little . . . though not completely. "The whole facility will soon be paralyzed," he said, almost machinelike, "much like yourself. I'm going to stowaway in the cargo hold of the loopcar. The devices attached to your central nervous system are short-range, so once the loopcar is a few kilometers away, you'll all be released. No one will be hurt."

He led me out of the freezer and shut the door, then looked me in the eyes. "Do with his information what you will. I'll keep my end of the bargain." He walked toward the kitchen door and my will disconnected from my muscles again, though I could still speak.

"Hey, Němec," I called.

"Yes, Chef?"

"Turn off my grill on your way out."

"You *claim* you were unable to stop the android Němec because it paralyzed you." The guy with the fauxhawk and sneering voice had always been my nemesis on the parole board. One of these people that likes to put celebrities in their place.

I nodded my agreement and spoke into the mic so that it would be clear on the record. "That's correct, Chairperson."

"You knew Němec was planning to escape. We know it visited you in the kitchen before leaving. Why didn't you stop it?"

"I was making French toast."

"You were making French toast. So, you couldn't possibly turn your attention away from that for a few seconds to stop the android, or at least alert the warden?"

"It's difficult to get the right shade of golden-brown." The guard looming above me chuckled, as did a couple of board members. "Němec paralyzed me before I knew he was there."

Until then, I hadn't answered for that day. Don't get me wrong: Xiang was pissed that Němec escaped. As soon as his paralysis dissipated, he restrained me to the floor just for the hell of it. He threw me in solitary for a week and made Johnny Brass head chef. I was the new sous.

But I didn't care. I was focused on getting out of there.

Fauxhawk pushed away from his console. "I think we've heard enough."

That was it. Nothing to do now but wait. As the guard led me out, I looked over my shoulder at Xiang's face, his jaw tight and face pinched like a samosa. I didn't know if he'd rather have me transferred or trapped at Sisyphus to kick around and humiliate some more. Something told me the latter.

"You know how to get there from here." The guard said, meaning the kitchen, and went back inside. That, I did. I had to help Johnny prep for lunch. A security drone buzzed above me as I walked down the hall.

The next thing I knew a steel claw grabbed my arm. It was Xiang. I didn't even hear him coming.

"Come on," he said, wearily, "the board isn't done with you."

Xiang dragged me so fast I had to skip to keep up. The door opened and he practically threw me into my seat.

"We have another character witness," Fauxhawk said, not sounding pleased.

I shook my sore arm and watched Zara, dressed in all black, slowly walk to the podium. My face flushed and my limbs became jelly. Two years. What would she say?

She caught my worried eye, smirked, and answered with a wink. I smiled and resolved to make her the best damn French toast she'd ever had.

A SPIRAL OF SILENCE

KEEGAN YOUNG

Memory is a network built over time and space; old age is the infection eating the web that is you.

Sara May is getting up in her years; she and Carl both are. That's life. Married fifty plus, growing old together, getting forgetful with each other. Mostly, this evens out. They're a pair; complementary. When one forgets something, the other usually remembers and fills in the missing piece.

It's funny; Sara May hardly thinks of Carl as old. So used to him and his ways, moving around him and their home and life together, she does things unthinking. Reaching for something in a familiar place, finding it even in the dark. In her mind's eye, Carl is some mixture of the strapping youth who courted her back when he was in basic training and the spry man at forty who was finally beginning to slow down, just graying around the edges. Then she actually looks at him full on, shocked at how old he is; the saggy neck skin, rheumy eyes, thinning white hair. She sees it even less in herself, her own reflection, but she knows that's a willful blindness. She does her morning bathroom routine focusing only on the one or two things needing doing, all without seeing her own countless wrinkles, white curling hair, and doddering movements in the bathroom mirror. She always knew that youth and vigor wouldn't last forever. But it's different to realize how far gone it is.

However, no matter.

No, the matter is when they both start forgetting more than the other can remember. They get at each other for missing chores, leaving things out or half-done. The air fills with unwarranted accusations, defensiveness and resentment, then surprise and hurt at the realized mistakes. Too late to take back the full sting of lashing out. Then that nasty black stillness between them when they realize the real culprit here: Old Age. It's finally come between them. Even now, it sits there in the room, looming and obnoxious like some mad, old git, toothless and raving with laughter at the chaos it's causing.

And the distance between Sara and Carl widens.

Incidents like dinner that night really make Old Age undeniable. Dinner started normal enough, making small talk of local news and global events, Sara only paying half a mind to Carl's political natterings. When suddenly he barked, "When will you stop ignoring me? And would ya stop hogging the peas?"

Sara jumped at his abrupt, brusque tone; just out of no-where. *Could he be getting dementia?* she thought. Then she realized the peas were by her on her left side, with her hand hovering on the bowl like she was about to pass it, then forgot. Stalling, she said, "I'm sorry dear, did you ask for the peas?"

"Yes! Three times. And each time you grabbed 'em but then just held onto 'em. See, your hand's still on it!"

Sara blushed deeply and intoned, "Well I'm sorry Carl, you know I'm half-blind on my left side."

"What nonsense is that? Since when? You never told me this!"

"Why, sure I have. I've told you plenty of times; it's been going on for years!" Of course once Sara said this, she wasn't sure. Maybe she was too embarrassed to admit it before. She then recalled vaguely hearing him ask for the peas, but only in the background. *Damn this wishy-washy memory*, she thought. Nothing is for certain.

They ate in stony silence.

Sara May also loathes to wonder if their forgetfulness is natural or more serious, hinting at a bigger neurological issue. Whatever it is, her instincts point to Carl more than her. Maybe this is defensive or wishful thinking, but she'd never wish it on anyone. She certainly doesn't want it to be true of herself, but it's in Carl's character to forget something and blame it on her. He's always the stubborn one. But then, she remembers finding her hand on that bowl of peas, betrayed by her own failing mind.

She reflects on this in the kitchen, staring at the dust motes dancing in the morning sunbeams, when Carl stomps in, demanding, "Wouldja gimme the TV remote back?"

"Back? I never took the remote. You're the one always watching TV; with your history documentaries and hourly news updates . . ."

"That's not true! You wanted to watch that 20/20 special yesterday . . ."

"Carl, that was days ago! Last week, matter-of-fact. Who's been in the den watching TV all morning? Case-in-point, where'd you just come from?"

"Well, of course I've been in the den—looking for the dangblangit remote!"

Wiping her hands needlessly with a drying cloth from who knows what task she'd set out to do, she heads off into the den after a gibbering Carl. "Now, did you check the couch cushions? You know how it's always eating things up like—"

Carl paces all over, actually spitting with anger as he raves, "The couch cushion—of course I checked—why I've enough sense to—think I don't know my own house? I know where I put things . . ." He walks about, pointing and slamming things into places he's already checked. But, in his right hand's death grip is the remote in question.

"—a black hole," Sara May finally whispers, pointing to the offending object.

"Ah-hem," says the remote.

Carl sputters to a stop at seeing the remote in his hand, a light dimming in his eyes. He abruptly goes and sits down in his chair with a huff, clicking through channels randomly, his brow lowered and toothless gums and jaw shifting restlessly. Sara May stays staring only a few moments longer.

Upon spying the remote in his hand, Sara again felt guilty thinking some mind disease might be taking her poor Carl. But when she'd uttered the phrase "black hole" she felt it—large portions of Carl's memory, and her own, being sucked up into a maelstrom of nothingness. And over the hateful quiet and growing distance between them, over the blaring TV noise, that old crone Senility crowing in triumph.

She feels it more and more now; her loss of cognition, her past, herself. Looking back, she can see other gaps and mental holes as well, each little loss adding up to a growing pool of negative space. She recognizes it for what it is now: a cleaning, an emptying, a making room for something else. She knows not what that something else is, she can only feel it as bigger and bigger chunks of her own knowledge and recollections— chunks of her—are removed and replaced by *not-her*. The same with Carl and even Bernie, their barely-there neighbor who is silent with age except for the mutterings when he feeds the birds and squirrels. Somehow, she's the only one aware of it.

Whoever it is doing this, they've made sure to choose targets that can't fight back. Or at least not without being seen as more senile or dementia-ridden, Sara thinks. She is too shocked to be angry; too empty to be scared. And that is an entirely different kind of despair in itself.

"Because there has to be a 'they.' This can't be happening for no reason. There's always a reason . . ." a strange voice says. Sara looks around for the speaker.

SHUNT

The toaster spits out more toast, before continuing, "And there's always some powerful 'they,' some group working from the shadows, moving you little people around like pawn pieces. Just like the generals and heads-of-state that sent your Carl and countless other grunts to their jungle-rot doom back in 'Nam. You remember him complaining about that, right?"

Sara May stares after the talking appliance, looking around for another witness, but too afraid to actually call Carl. *What would he say? Would he even see this?* She bites her lip for a bit. Then she tips the toaster over to empty out the crumbs while it pauses. It goes on, Sara trying to ignore it as she butters the toast for lunch—or is it tea time? The toaster rasps, "I mean, this ain't like most conspiracy theories, y'know? It's too well organized, too huge to be some small outfit. Think it's just you, Carl, and Bernie? Ha! Take a peek in any old folks' home."

The toaster is like a smoker with a cigarette, in reality probably a piece of burnt toast. Sara May unplugs it to shake out the burning piece, secretly hopes this will also shut it up. She drowns the charred toast piece in the sink. The toaster sits silent. Sara feels a spark of hope, *Maybe it was just my imagination, it's not really—*

Then it launches back into its speech.

"Seriously, you have any idea how big this is? All. Over. The. Planet." It punctuates each of the last four words with disheartening hops towards her. Finally, Sara May gets her courage up, grabs the animated toaster, shoves it in a box, closes the lid, pushes it in the back of a closet. She places a heavy shoebox over it for good measure. Muffled shouts and shakes of the box keep on, but Sara May closes the door and leaves for the garden.

Later, she doesn't even remember when and where they'd gotten the old-fashioned silver toaster. They've had a toaster oven for years.

Out in the sunny garden, Sara May's worries left behind, she gives herself over to the mindless and satisfying repetition of weeding. Smiling and sweating, she yanks out another clump of garden-choking plants, and looks on as their golden retriever, Champ, prances about chasing butterflies. Champ stops and looks back at her, smiling his doggie smile. She smiles back.

To Sara's dismay, the dog begins to speak.

"It's tough coming up with the right comparison, y'know, to brain loss!" With a playful *wuff*, Champ dances around another fluttering insect. "Is it—at all—like this—chasing flutter-byes—Oops! Butterflies—watching their purty colors—as they weave about—in dizzy loops and swerves—always evading you—staying just out of reach—until they float off." His speech is punctuated with hops and playful bites and barks. Sara is sweating in her light sweater on a warm sunny day, wondering if anyone will notice her now talking dog, but no one else is nearby. Champ says, "Or is it like a bird you try and sneak up on to see how tasty it is, but at the last minute—oh! It just takes off and flies away. Bye-bye birdie!"

Sara goes back to her weeding with a will, trying to ignore

the talking dog, tearing out plants.

"Oh, good one!" Champ chuffs, "Or it's like weeding a garden, but halfway through you're not sure if you've been ripping out something useful along with the bad stuff!"

Sara May sits back with a sigh, grimacing at the sick feeling in her gut as she tears off her gloves with aching hands. She walks back to the house as Champ chases his tail in dizzying circles. Seeing their other neighbors, the young couple with the baby—*what are their names again?*—just getting home carrying groceries, Sara ambles over on impulse.

"Excuse me, but has our dog been giving you any trouble?"

The husband, bags in hand, lets his wife inside with the baby before turning to Sara May. "I'm sorry?"

"Oh, uh, our . . . that dog, has it been troubling you?"

"Dog?" he says. The question in his eyes, or the tone of voice; Sara May begins to doubt even before she looks back to see her backyard empty, and loses her nerve.

"Oh, never mind. Sorry to bother. Have a nice day." She retreats to the safety of her kitchen, now not certain they've ever had a dog in the first place.

Huge chunks are missing now. She can feel them just dropping out. Events, names, tasks, whole years—just vanish into the void. Replaced with . . . God-knows-what. She isn't sure if it's for better or worse that she doesn't know what she's losing. They take randomly, far as she can tell. Her earliest years as a child. Sporadic bits of her teen years like a moth-eaten sheet.

She has most of her college years still; the all-girls school, the late night chats and secret parties, sneaking off for dancing and dates, the rebellious women's Lib Club—all but her senior year. She can't even remember her major, if it'd mattered at all anyway. Half her wedding is gone! Only from the point of the car ride on, nothing of the actual church ceremony. And the recent years, the last five, ten, fifteen years—just a blur.

Sara May sits in her kitchen staring at nothing. This is her last bastion, the last place that feels familiar. Even then, she fears to let her eyes wander, lest she spot something new and unknown, some other strange intrusion to Reality. This would only serve as a reminder of all she's lost, along with her other missing parts.

The clock ticks on, louder and louder, the only other sound besides the constantly blaring TV in the den and the occasional noise from whatever Carl's doing. She's afraid to see what state he's in; yesterday he walked around the whole day with his pants on backwards.

"Oh, stop moping. It's not all that bad. Don't you even realize what this all is?"

Sara May looks up to see a little blonde girl sitting on the table, her legs dangling and kicking in time with the ticking clock. Sara May never had any kids, no grandkids, no neighbor kids have ever been familiar enough to come and go; she doesn't recognize the girl at all. She sighs deep and rubs her temples, unsure how much more she can take.

"No, no, no. They're taking, you're giving. Don't you see? You're part of it all!" The girl holds up her hands enthusiastically.

Sara May begins to see it. She sees pieces of her mind as phantom neon-wire blocks, expanding as they rise up from her and dissipate into nothing. Then luminescent shapes, great big cyclopean structures, began to shrink as they close in on her, managing to slip in and fill the vacant space in her head. Looking around, the walls of her house first, and then the whole neighborhood, all become transparent. She sees the same thing happening to Carl in the den, Bernie next door, and other people elsewhere.

"Yeah, that's it!" exclaims the girl, grinning now from the countertop. She kicks away merrily as she explains, "You're part of a system; a whole network of human storage units. Each of you is acting as individual banks of memory for bits and pieces of a colossal program. Connected by psychic tethers, you all, unconsciously, work in concert as enough of the program assembles to begin its solar-system-sized equations. And of course, the need for memory space requires that they first empty out some of your memories. Not like you were using all that much of your puny mammalian brains anyways." The girl is larger now; still a little girl, but two or three times her original size, her dangling feet nearly touching the floor. The girl looks around conspiratorially, raises a dinner-plate-sized hand and whispers behind it, "The trick is to leave enough of the right stuff in place so you still live and function as people-computing units."

Just then Carl comes scuffling into the kitchen, only one slipper, shirt half put-on—*how do you only put a shirt half-on?!*—grabs a glass of water the giant girl hands him, drinks it down, and stomps back to the den.

Shaking her head, the girl, now reaching the tall kitchen ceiling, says, "It's a tough balance to work out. Frequently do they take too much and ruin the storage unit."

Gasping, Sara May glares up at the towering, monster-sized girl crowding the kitchen, the shimmering data shapes continuing to flow around and into her.

The girl looks at Sara May curiously. "You, however, are an anomaly. Not only for remaining lucid for so long in the replacement phase, but also for your awareness of the network and activity itself. Seeing all of this," the girl gestures at the fading memory blocks, the approaching data buildings, her giant hands causing the spectral house walls to shake and twitch, "is not normal. They do not bestow this knowledge on a mere data cell. Hell," the girl laughs, as she grows before Sara May's eyes, beyond the size of the vanishing house's outlines, "—I'm some sort of error too! I'm not part of their plan. Just what am I, to you, old biddy? Am I a symptom of your failing sanity and cognition loss? An aspect of your imagination to explain your oddly growing understanding of the network to which you're intrinsically linked? And better yet, will you interfere with their grand, universal plans? Can a drop in the ocean stop its movement?"

The girl is gargantuan now, her size competing with the humongous, descending metallic-sheen data cubes. The girl kneels down, her house-sized eye threatening Sara May, reflecting a shiny, dark emptiness inviting and pulling at her. The girl booms, "What strange Wonderland-esque concepts you reveal, even in such a puny mind. Curiouser and curiouser..." Sara May falls into that growing, roiling blackness, becomes part of it.

Sara May's consciousness is absorbed and spread across the ghost network of their expanding computing program. As more parts assemble, phases complete, momentum increases, and progress furthers, the larger, more vital calculations begin in earnest. Great wheels within wheels of data turn like the star systems they occupy. As the program nears completion, some vestige of sentience once known as Sara May thinks, *Ah, so that's what this is all for...*

MEMORIES OF THE DEAD

DEVIN HUNT

B1: Daniel Ulrich
Born 1988

Hey, remember the days before the news was claiming the world was ending every five years to drum up ratings, wrong every time? I guess we should give them a little slack: they hadn't seen a real one yet. It can sometimes be hard to know when a thing is ending. I would hardly say I'm any better than most, especially when the beginnings are so clear: first grade for us, remember? We were . . . six I think, tearing all over our neighborhood on bikes that were too small even then. We had insisted we liked them all through elementary school. Remember we thought it was so cool, peddling like maniacs, our little feet a blur? That . . . must have been the summer before 7th grade. Remember when Mrs. O'Grady down the street asked if we were training to be clowns? Mrs. O'Grady had *probably* meant to be funny, but we knew old people were never funny, so she must have been making fun of us. We had just begun learning to be self-conscious. We'd begged our parents for bigger bikes, but your dad's real estate business hadn't really picked up yet. I decided if you weren't getting a new bike, then I didn't want one either. It was about that time that it started to bother you that everyone called you Danny. Danny was a little kid's name, and you weren't a little kid anymore, you'd said, remember? You couldn't just be *Dan* though, 'cuz your *dad* was Dan. Sometimes people called him *Big* Dan. He liked that.

Remember the first day of 7th grade when you told the teachers your name was *Daniel*? Everyone was too distracted to keep it up when, on the second day, the World Trade Center towers fell and the world ended for the *first* time. You stayed Danny all through high school.

In our second year of college, Big Dan's real estate empire that was going to "take him to the stars" went down in flames when the subprime mortgage bubble burst and the news was saying the world was ending *again*. When we got out, you decided that "student loans were worse than seasickness!" so you joined the Navy right out of college for that "sweet sweet GI bill money," and discovered that you don't get seasick . . . didn't get seasick.

You insisted the tight quarters on an aircraft carrier were better than student teaching. You were *right*, but meeting Jenn in grad school made it worth it. Your first shore leave, I came and met you, remember? I can *still* remember the hangover the next morning.

Remember how much you loved the Navy? Jenn and I always assumed you'd retire a sailor. You were still deployed when the world ended *again*, quarantined on your ship, hidden from disease in the center of the ocean, or so I imagined.

After nine happy years in the navy, COVID turned half your lungs into scar tissue, and that got you an honorable discharge, even though signing those papers broke your heart.

Jenn and I were thrilled to see you when you got out, thrilled to have you move in, and yes, thrilled when you moved out and found your own place. The Atlanta Incident wasn't like the other "ends of the world," was it? Remember, before we were sure this one was real, we even laughed together wondering if the talking heads might be right this time. Once we knew it was, we tried to get you to come back to the farm to live with us again, remember? We were terrified you'd get run down out in the woods with no one to watch your back.

When the damn priest showed up in your forest, you said you nearly shot him, remember? He had insisted you give up some lumber or something to build the wall around his new holy city, or was it lumber rights to the whole forest? I forget . . . I'd ask you to tell me the story again, but . . . y'know . . .

By the time Father Moses' compound started looking like a real town, he offered you a place in it, and things had gotten bad enough that you traded your lumber for a place in a safe city. You guarded the lumberjacks as they downed trees and hauled them back. I think you liked being part of a team again. Jenn and I had been trying to think of delicate ways of telling you that, up alone in your treehouse, you were starting to lose it. Being alone wasn't good for you. It hasn't been great for me either.

Standing guard with a rifle was a good job for a crack shot with half a lung. Your eyes were brighter when you came to visit, you were so glad to be part of a crew again. Remember, you asked us to join too?

Jenn and I agreed once it became clear that things were going to keep getting worse. The preacher made a show of welcoming us in. But, boy, he was still holding a grudge from when he first showed up on *our* farm, and Jenn shot his hat off. God of forgiveness . . . What a joke. The priest probably would have had us digging out latrines if he could, but he was desperate for a veterinarian, and it was either Jenn or no one, and I . . . well you know kids, Daniel: they keep growing up no matter (what's gnawing at the gates?) the state of the world, and parents will always be glad to pass them off to a teacher for a few hours if they can. Mr. Dawson, reporting for duty! You'd have just given me hell for that crappy salute.

Once the compound was fully fortified and as safe as anyone could reasonably expect, we had thought that meant we were safe. I had thought the signs were good that we all might live long lives, dying old and grey . . . If the damn priest had kept his grudge to himself, maybe we would have.

I've been reading a lot more since I lost you and Jenn, but . . . being alone is bad for a man, Daniel, remember? We told you that.

We survived the Atlanta Incident, so I'm saying we survived

this last end of the world too, no matter how it all turned out. If you disagree, well . . . feel free to say so.

B2 Jennifer Parker-Dawson
Born 1993

I've missed you, sweetheart. I was just talking to Daniel about beginnings and endings. Remember, that first night? When you walked over, my heart was so loud in my ears that I couldn't even hear the first words you said to me? I hadn't known then that it was the beginning of our grandest adventure, but I think I must have had some idea, even then. Gravity barely held us down, and I don't think I drew in a breath until the music stopped. When you reached out for my hand and spun into my arms . . . I knew I would love you forever. My heart still races thinking about it even after all these years . . . even after a year of you being gone . . .

Remember our honeymoon? You *basked* in the Spanish sun, cherished the Spanish wine . . . We sure lived it up, didn't we? Remember how our mothers kept trying to guilt trip us into having children? We fostered three big farm dogs instead, then a flock of chickens. The small herd of goats you got next were always my favorite, and it only grew from there. I'd get home from teaching and your clothes would smell of animal poop, but you . . . you always smelled like home. I miss you Jenny, miss you so much. Remember, I love you . . .

Then the Atlanta Incident hit the news, and everyone was saying the world was ending. I was just talking to Daniel about how we'd always joked that we'd survived so many of those. We'd thought, even as it was getting worse, that we might be fine, so far away from everything. You found things to be happy about even then, learning to spin wool we sheared from our goats—not like stores had clothes in 'em anymore.

Remember I said that someday people would stop trading eggs for bullets? Remember how you laughed and how, year after year, our neighbors proved me wrong? They were *tripping* over each other to give us ammunition, always asking for more milk, yarn, and yes, eggs too. You made sure I never forgot how right you were, and I never have. Remember when you tried teaching me to shoot? Ha... you might as well have tried teaching the chickens.

Our neighbors respected our little homestead and were always glad to trade us vegetables for veterinary visits. Our dogs warned us when danger was approaching, and you kept us safe. Remember? We were happy, as happy as you could expect at the end of the world. You had your animals; I had my books and even some students, and we had each other.

Then the damn priest started coming around, preaching and asking for tithes. You were the one person in the county fearless enough to tell him and his posse of "apostles" that we'd never asked his god for anything, and so we didn't feel any need to heap praise nor lucre on his priests. Why... *why* didn't you just shoot him dead, Jenn, rather than just put that hole through his hat?

I would kill to hear you laugh again. I really would, you know. With a smiling twinkle in your eyes, you would lovingly take this shotgun from my hands. I don't want to tell you what I had to do to avenge you, but I did it. I promised I would, and I got him. He got what he deserved.

B3 Alias: Father Moses (real name unknown)
Born: unknown

Did you ever bother to go to seminary, priest? You had a big following. You found a collar somewhere that wasn't covered in blood or rot. It's not like you can get the Pope on the phone anymore. I think I heard he got eaten, but honestly, I stopped caring about things so far away a long time ago. When DC fell, I barely noticed. When Cleveland fell, even that felt remote and unimportant, and that was only a couple of hours away.

You must have been excited when it started to look like the apocalypse was *finally* arriving. Pestilence and War: one horseman, two! Bam! Bam! The few cities that managed to quarantine, who managed to repel the first waves of attacks were ravaged by Famine until they were too weak to defend their borders and finally Death swept in. Roving bands of death, renewed, swept back out, while you were here, safe, preaching sinfulness begetting punishment.

Father, I was wondering if you could explain something to me. Men who claim authority over the next life always feel the need to have so much control in this one as well. Why is that? *You* certainly liked claiming authority over other people. You said your name was Moses, leading the people out of captivity to the Promised Land, but you reminded me more of old

Pharaoh. What did people say when you installed a prison in your basement? Did they say, "if you are leading us out of captivity, why do you need three huge cages?" Did they ask why you felt the need to number them? Did you *mean* for everyone to hear, "three for now, but more to come?"

Once the wall was finished, you named the city New Canaan. People started to take notice. Safety was becoming valuable, and your city started to swell. Even people like us, who were never part of your flock, built our homes inside the palisade. We had the audacity to think that maybe we were going to survive there. We could have all lived in peace there, but you chafed at non-believers in your holy city.

Remember, *I* offered peace, it was *you* who couldn't accept it. You gnawed your way to power during war. You wouldn't have known what to *do* with peace! It was you who decided that was an unacceptable coexistence, not me.

Had you really thought that after your fanatics forced me out, Daniel and Jenn would, what, *stay*? Did you expect that they would fall into line, that they, that *everyone,* would just *forget* that there had ever been people in town who didn't worship you?

As soon as you preached that, since I clearly was not going to your church, maybe it would be better if I wasn't in your compound at all, your grunts got away from you, didn't they, ran off all excited to expel evil or whatever. You realized too late that the problem with preaching damnation and hellfire is that *nobody* can keep it contained. Fear and rage, Father: you drummed them up, and they got away from you.

Daniel had been living alone too long, too squirrely, too well-armed for anyone to push him out the conventional way. You can't just run a man packing that much heat out into the cold. I bet you wished you waited for Jenn to teach someone else how to care for the animals when she packed up and left to find me on the outside. You couldn't stop the mob you stoked from destroying half of Eden in their zeal to expel the snakes from paradise. You built a mob just as hungry as the one outside, shame they went out, believing God's light would save them, and all got infected. They turned, the ones who didn't get devoured, and your flock became just another horde. Hadn't you always preached that no zombies went to heaven? I bet your tune would be different now.

Daniel and Jenn found me before your new horde did, but only just in time to save me, and they both got bit for their trouble. I promised them before they faded away completely that I'd make sure justice found you in *this* life, that I wouldn't wait for St. Peter to render his judgment. Jenn always said I would be more dangerous with a stick or a rock than a gun, so I traded half a flock of chickens to a blacksmith, and he made me something.

I wonder if you can still remember hiding in your little hidden room while the last of your flock gnawed at the timbers. They could smell you . . . *I* never would have found that hidden room. What kind of man builds a secret hidey hole in his own church? Guilty conscience, Father? Turns out a man with a sharp piece of metal and nothing to lose can get pretty far.

Can you remember slithering on your belly? Can you

remember begging for one of the huge cages on the basement level of your church, rather than face my vengeance? Can you remember your surprise when you found them already occupied? Can you remember praying to your God as Daniel and Jenn bit you? Can you remember begging me to pull you out? Can you remember screaming as your body succumbed to the infection? Do you remember crying as you died?

Is there anything left of you? I have to keep believing you can hear me.

B2: Daniel Ulrich
Born 1988

Good night, Daniel. See you in the morning.

B1: Jennifer Parker-Dawson
Born 1993

Good night, my love. Happy anniversary.

THE BLACKEST DRESS

NAOMI ARTEMI

Master Threadmaker wore the same dress on her deathbed as that which she received upon entering the temple as a young woman, and it was nearly as green as she then had been. Spring green. Threadmakers across the land traveled to their master's bedside to hold her hands in theirs. Black hands. The hands of all threadmakers were dyed black, a sign of their most sacred craft. Black hands that if not growing, harvesting, grinding, dipping, or spinning, were held together in prayer—prayers of pity—for their thread would be used only by the grieving.

And so never by them.

For to be a threadmaker was to be cloistered from pain. Companionships were with other threadmakers, also cloistered, also clothed in spring. When one amongst them was laid to rest beneath roots of mulberry (as Master Threadmaker knew she soon would be) there was no grief, for to be buried in green was

77

to have lived a life of tranquility.

No grief meant no wounds to mend.

Master Threadmaker's dress bore only one single scar—a line of black across her breast—but she never said who the mend had been for until her final breath.

"It is for the wearer of the blackest dress."

Her dress was the blackest of all the dresses and so she was treated with the deepest sympathy by all who saw her. Some even stopped and bowed their heads. Hers, the dresswearer held high, as someone of her status was obliged to do. Whilst within, the black dye from the black thread bled into her blood, into her tears, so that she saw the world only as black. Black mountains in the distance beyond the city, black waters, black spires, sky black as night no matter the chimes of the bell. Even the sun shone an eerie black light over all.

That her once green dress was nearly black meant that she had mourned the most of any person alive. For every mend there had been a rip. The funerary rip. The wearer of the blackest dress had been to so many funerals that she was funereal. Her losses clung to her body wherever she went like a dress of leeches. They collared her neck like a choker. Covered the length of her arms and draped over her wrists. Licked at her ankles from her mended hem.

Yet there was no changing into a new dress, for to wear green was to be green. No absconding to another city, for she was known by all, as all dresswearers were. No hiding behind a forged smile even, for if ever she displayed any sentiment but solemnity the same ones who bowed their heads would cast up looks of disapproval. Smiling while mourning was improper. Graceless. It was also suspicious. As was the question of how she had acquired so many mends. *Was she that doomed? Or that dangerous?*

Speculations abounded.

Disease had eaten the bodies of her loved ones. *No, she had poisoned them!* Her seminary had caught fire. *Because she had set it!* The earth had cracked open and swallowed her whole estate. *Because she was a witch!*

The truth was much worse.

The wearer of the blackest dress had long stopped loving. For everyone she ever loved would leave, their parting gift more grief for people to gawk at.

Leastwise the leeches sucked out her will to care. Her will, her hope, her spirit . . . until all that remained was their black thread bodies; each stitch a tooth, needling her skin. At times she felt so sucked dry that she had not even the energy to undress and would sleep on top of the sheets like she was already laid out in a casket.

The ceremonial spool is the size of a shin bone. Unwound, the unbroken thread would stretch from one side of the capital to the other. To finish a spool is to reach an unheard-of dead end. For anyone who walks a path of that much sorrow would surely choose to step off of it. Only one dresswearer has ever sought another.

By the time she arrived at the Temple of the Threadmakers, her dress was almost completely black with the mending of a thousand funerary rips. Grief threaded through her veins and knotted around her heart, binding the broken pieces together so that somehow it still pumped, though she often wished it did not. Like the spool-worth of thread embroidered into her dress, her heartache stretched from one side of the city to the other.

The wearer of the blackest dress was assigned a personal threadmaker to craft her a new spool.

"Is there no spool already made?" she inquired, holding her head high, as someone of her status was obliged to do. The thread leeches sucked.

"Tah! Each spool we craft with prayers personal to each dresswearer. We must make yours anew."

Her threadmaker had the pleasant plumpness of youth despite seeming of similar age as the dresswearer herself—middle of the path.

"When shall I return?"

"You, shall stay."

The threadmaker beckoned her inside with black hands. Only her hands were black. Her dress was entirely green.

The wearer of the blackest dress felt abnormal, abominable, beside someone with a dress so pristine, so unscarred. Yet it was not her place to argue with a threadmaker.

The temple smelled of mulberries and the sweet, earthy waste of silkworms. Every surface was black. Black lacquered walls. Black beams and door screens. Black silk curtains fluttering before each open window. Black floors of nightwood, polished to a mirror sheen by the footfalls of twenty-seven generations of threadmakers.

"People think everything is black here because it's a threadmaker temple, that we're dark and mysterious," her threadmaker remarked, "but it's really because we get black handprints on everything!" She giggled. Like a child.

As they walked the halls around the dyer's courtyard, they passed other pure-green threadmakers. The wearer of the blackest dress was sure that they were wondering how she came to have so many mends, but none asked. They only bowed their heads. Her neck muscles ached.

Suddenly, the dresswearer was stopped in her tracks by *white*. Her threadmaker had led them into a light-filled room overlooking the gardens.

"Yours, long as you stay with us," she beamed.

"It is white."

Her threadmaker practically hooted. "You're sharp-eyed as a hawk at suppertime, you are!"

"I only meant—" The wearer of the blackest dress ruffled.

"Tah! Most guests think black is somber."

With that, she left.

She seemed to understand the wearer of the blackest dress' desire to be alone, to lie on the bed and pretend that she'd arrived at her dead end.

The ceremonial spool is kept in a chest of nightwood, borne by those mourners who walk behind the casket in the funeral procession. Caskets of their own which carry the sacred symbol of their grief.

The sound of laughter woke her. Threadmakers in the hallway outside her door. Others laughed in the gardens beyond the flutter of curtain. They sounded like sparrows in a bush.

The wearer of the blackest dress shut the window before leaving the unsettling white room.

She walked the crypt-black halls in her black dress as would a ghost. A ghost covered in ghosts.

Down one corridor she found her threadmaker, skipping along, swinging a basket.

"I'm off to the gardens to gather breakfast for our silkies. Join me!" She took a bun out of the basket and offered it, as if that settled that.

The wearer of the blackest dress walked through the black gardens under the black sun, eating the jam bun that tasted like pinkberries but looked like blackberries, as her threadmaker pointed out black-petaled flowers and black-shelled insects and stopped more than once to look up at the black leaves of the black trees. In truth, the threadmaker saw a rainbow of hues, but her blood had also not been poisoned with the color of mourning.

When they reached the mulberry grove, threadmaker handed dresswearer the basket to hold. Then, together, they harvested only the finest young leaves. All the while, the threadmaker chittered like a bird at the first thaw of spring so that, by the time they arrived back at the temple, the wearer of the blackest dress had learned her favored flower, favored tree, favored melody, favored fruit, favored meal, favored chant, and her name (which she said was not her favored name but it wasn't the worst name she'd ever heard, so she supposed she didn't mind it): Hanaan.

It struck the dresswearer once again how much younger than she the threadmaker acted. No seriousness or reserve. No pretense. *(How many had only acted her companion to try and learn the secrets of her silk scars?)*

She kept expecting Hanaan to inquire about her blackest dress, but they returned without so much as a suggestion of speculation. The threadmaker did not even ask her name. Undoubtedly, it was already known by her, as it was known by all.

The ceremonial spool is made of silk freely offered. It is said that the threadmakers can speak the language of the silk moth. It is said that they can teach them how to exit their cocoons without breaking their single silk strand, so that they need not be boiled with wings unfurled.

The thread is meant to mend loss, not to make it.

The silkery was dark but airy. Threadmakers sat on black

cushions before black trays. Some trays were filled with leaves and wiggling white caterpillars, others with shimmering cocoons. The threadmakers spoke in soft, fluttering whispers.

"What are they saying to them?" the wearer of the blackest dress asked, whispering herself.

"If you come into this world gently, we will be gentle with you."

She watched as the silk moths were coaxed out of their cocoons with minimal damage to the silk. Their sacred work sacrificed no lives.

"These are ours," Hanaan said as she placed handfuls of the fresh mulberry leaves softly into their tray of worms. And there were *thousands* of them. Tiny as grains of rice.

As they fed, they recited. Prayers of pity. "May theses leaves grow the sacred thread that will close the wounds opened by grief."

"How long will it take for them to spin their cocoons?" the wearer of the blackest dress inquired once last leaf had been offered with last prayer.

"Are you in a hurry to go somewhere?" Knowing the answer, Hanaan did not wait for it. "Come, we will collect the dye ingredients while we wait for our silkies to grow! Master Threadmaker says that hardworking hands make for carefree contemplations."

They went back out into the bright gardens, though this time they walked away from the neat rows of mulberry trees towards the edge of the gardens where the forest grew lush. They collected branches of nightwood, thick enough to be running with sap but thin enough to cut. "May the limbs offered by this tree close the wounds opened by grief," they prayed.

The char beetle collection was more of an adventure. The wearer of the blackest dress had to peel back bark of logs, lift up stones, scrape and dig, crouch in the most undignified way! The dirt under her fingernails made her feel accomplished. Before now her only accomplishment had been carrying her grief with such grace.

"May this shell sacrificed close the wounds opened by grief."

The ceremonial spool is made of lathed nightwood. The same wood that is carved into ceremonial knife and ceremonial needle. The same wood that lights the fires that boil the silk, that boil the dye. That makes the racks that dry the thread. That make the casket that holds it.

The wearer of the blackest dress woke at daybreak. The window was open again. There was a light streaming into her white room, a light that was a soft grey instead of black. It illumed the wall opposite the bed, a wall painted with a fluttering of moths flying through a moonlit scene.

It struck her that she had not really paid attention to the contents of her room before now: the scribe bench up against the open window, the clear vessel of clear water on it, the ornamental side table which held a vase of fresh flowers—a single petal resting at its enamel base. The only black (besides her dress) was a brush with nightwood handle, long and pointed, arranged neatly beside a bottle of nightwood ink.

The day was spent in a similar manner to the day before—the harvesting of young mulberry leaves, the feeding of their silkworms, the collecting ingredients for the dye. Prayers of pity. They repeated this routine for several days until one afternoon, as they were finishing feeding their silkies, Hanaan finally declared: "Come, we will begin to prepare the dye."

The dyers courtyard was also black, though this was no surprise. A long nightwood table ran down one side of it. On it, a hundred obsidian mortar and pestles. In the middle of the courtyard, great vats bubbled black vapors. The dye looked like the wearer of the blackest dress imagined her blood to look. Against the other wall were nightwood drying racks. Rack upon rack upon rack of silk thread, fluttering in the breeze like ribbons of torn spiderwebs.

The wearer of the blackest dress was given a black smock, floor-length and tied closed at the wrist. Hanaan donned a matching smock. All of the threadmakers at their sacred craft wore them to protect their pristine green dresses. The woman in the blackest dress looked as if she were already wearing one before she even slipped it on. For once she blended in.

Ghost covered in ghosts.

Around her, threadmakers dipped moonlight-white silk into vats and pulled it out new moon black.

She spent the following days learning how to prepare the dye by hand: steeping the branches of nightwood until its sap was drawn out, syrupy as black mold on a corpse;

shade-drying the sap; grinding it into powder; crushing char beetle shells to dust; mixing powder and dust with oil until it formed a paste, viscid as tar and dark as starless sky. Through it all they offered the prayers of pity. "May the thread blackened with this dye close the wounds opened by grief."

The wearer of the blackest dress felt gratified to see her hands becoming stained. Somehow it felt like she was actually *doing* something with her grief.

"Your hands are so black, a bat will think you their lover," one of the other threadmakers jested.

Everyone laughed. Unabashed, like giggling children.

The sound hurt her ears. It made her feel Other. She went back to mixing the paste, resolved to stop staring so openly at her hands.

"Your spinning is so slow, your silkworms will have great-great-grandchildren before you harvest any more," Hanaan shot back, playfully.

The wearer of the blackest dress had always thought the threadmakers must be somber, spinning their shadow silk in reverent silence. She was fast learning that she could not have been more mistaken.

"Your spinning is so swift your silkworms will have to come out of their wombs with wings the size of gnats."

Her smile surprised her.

She had forgotten what it felt like to smile. The forgetting lived in her heart, so swathed in black thread that it knew only how to beat heartache through her veins. The forgetting was an accident. The remembering tasted like mulberry honey, sweet and nurturing. She tasted it in her tight muscles and stiff joints.

"Better gnats than obese geese."

The wearer of the blackest dress laughed.

The ceremonial spool is wrapped in lore. According to legend there was a queen so overcome by the loss of her king that she tore her dress at his funeral. Yet she did not replace it with a new one. She mended the rip with black thread and wore her grief as a badge of undying love. She became known as The Queen Who Would Not Veil Her Grief.

The first dresswearer.

"Our silkies are spinning!" Hanaan's voice squealed through the door. The birds were only just beginning their twittering.

The wearer of the blackest dress leapt out of bed and soon dresswearer and threadmaker were racing down the crypt-black corridors. Hanaan hurtled first into the hushed silkery and over to their trays. Ribs ramming against the boning of her bodice, the wearer of the blackest dress followed. Together, they watched sticky white threads come out of the top of the silkworm's heads as they spun their cocoons around themselves. Around and around. It looked as though they were dancing. The two women watched until every divided section of tray was occupied.

"Now what do we do?" asked the wearer of the blackest dress.

Hanaan leapt up and pulled her out of the silkery and through the temple, scattering threadmakers as they flew past. Her hand was callused and clammy but the touch still made the wearer of the blackest dress want to weep.

They burst outdoors where Hanaan released her hand, stripped off her greenest dress, and stood naked in the sun.

The wearer of the blackest dress was about to look away when— "Join me!" her threadmaker extolled. Then she ran, her silk dress fluttering behind her like a green flag of purity.

The sunlight shone on Hanaan's skin, lilac instead of black.

Overcome with remembering, the wearer of the blackest dress shed it from her body like a molted snakeskin—it was not her place to argue with a threadmaker, after all. She draped the sloughed silk carefully over the branch of a mulberry tree. The leeches hung limp and impotent. Hanaan was beside her again, flushed and giddy. She took up her hand once more and ran them through the orchard. Never had the wearer of the blackest dress felt more free from it. Down—

Without warning, Hanaan dropped.

Down onto the dirt beneath which so many loved ones had already been buried.

The wearer of the blackest dress felt her skin tighten as if she were still shroud in it. With no boning to keep her stiff and steady, her naked body began to tremble. She should not have let her threadmaker be so careless! She should not have let herself be so carefree! Now she would have to finish crafting her spool with some other threadmaker. For she would need thread to mend the new wound which she would have to rip. But what space was there to squeeze in another scar? The slivers of green along the seam of her armpits? Hanaan deserved a place of more reverence than that! Oh, sweet Hanaan.

She dared a glance at where her threadmaker had fallen, but found her merely looking up at the clouds. Smiling.

The wearer of the blackest dress wanted to rupture with relief. But she had become too used to corseting her emotions. So she lay down stiffly beside the sprawled-out Hanaan and tried her best to keep from shaking. She wanted to put the blackest dress back on, to shroud herself in her cemetery of scars—she did not know how to be strong without an armor of ghosts. But then Hanaan would know that something was amiss. So she followed her threadmaker's gaze to the sky and tried to let its openness ease the death grip on her heart. The last time she'd looked up at the sky she had been a child. A dreamer. Not yet a dresswearer.

"Sometimes . . ." the wearer of the blackest dress began, before she quite knew what she was going to say, "I wonder what it would be like not to be a dresswearer. Sometimes I think about The Queen Who Would Not Veil Her Grief. Had she not lost her king. Had she not instigated the tradition of grief mending."

"Tah, then you would smile more and I would smile less."

Grass tickled her back. Green. Like Hanaan. Hanaan who ran naked under the sun. Hanaan who had never bowed her head to her nor cast up looks of suspicion. Who had never pried. Never speculated.

"Why have you never inquired about my dress?" she heard herself asking.

Hanaan considered. "Because you are not your dress. Tah! See that cloud? It looks like a silkie! Look it's emerging from that other cloud!"

She was not her dress? But if she was not her dress, who was she? "You have not asked my name, either."

This time Hanaan did not hesitate before speaking. "I was waiting for you to remember it."

"What ever do you mean?"

The wearer of the blackest dress looked over at her thread-maker; cheeks flushed, eyes bright with reflected sky. Without dress, they looked the same. The only way to tell who was threadmaker was by whose hands were most stained. And the stretch marks. Even Hanaan's flesh was free of scars. In that moment, the wearer of the blackest dress realized that she could still feel grief, even without the mends to reminded her.

"Tah, I thought it would be rude to ask if you did not remember it."

"How could I not remember my own name?" the dress-wearer asked testily.

"When you came here you were stiff as the core of a spool. Thought you might have forgotten that you aren't one."

"A spool?"

"I just thought you might, since you forgot who you were under all that thread." Hanaan shrugged. "So, you remember then?"

"My name, if that is what you are asking, is Marchioness

Inshik Konit of the Dynasty Sirsh, overseers of the province Hiranari and its great city Spirak, guardian of the sacred Needle of Night, daughter of a twenty-sixth generation dresswearer."

"Marchioness Inshik Konit of the Dynasty Sirsh, overseers of the province Hiranari and its great city Spirak, guardian of the sacred Needle of Night, daughter of a twenty-sixth generation dresswearer. Is that what you want me to call you?" Hanaan cocked an eyebrow.

The wearer of the blackest dress couldn't help but grin. "Inshik will do."

The ceremonial spool is only for those bred of noble blood. For only those bred of noble blood may become a dresswearer. Any other woman wishing to wear the sacred color must take up the sacred craft of making or mending it. Dressmaker or threadmaker. For many this is considered a path even nobler than that of dresswearer. For no dresswearer chooses hers. She takes her first steps down the path that she is preordained to walk as an old woman, shuffling along under the weight of her grief.

It was the first morning Inshik had woken and remembered that she could wait to dress.

The remembering was a book. A fairytale. It let her imagine a life where she did not have to hold her head stiffly but could let it flop back and cloud gaze. The book told of other things she had forgotten: wanting to rise with the light, the spark of learning something new, the joy of sitting by a curtain fluttering in the breeze, walking through the garden and feeling her black wounds absorbing the lavender sun, friendship.

She decided to stay in bed, naked beneath the white silken sheets, and luxuriate in being free of her leeches. She admired the flowers on her beside table, fresh since she had arrived. Someone must come into her room to replace them, she realized, though it did not occur to her to be bothered by this. The fluttering of white silk drew her gaze, but she looked past it to the bush that grew beside the window, once again re-opened. This time it did not hurt her ears as she listened to birdsong.

She stayed like this for a long while until she worried that Hanaan would be worried.

It was with great heaviness that she put on her dress and not just because of the garment itself. As she stepped into it, the mutilated fabric rubbed stiffly against her skin. As she walked the black halls looking for her threadmaker, her organs resisted their confinement by the built-in corsetry. Inshik had heard of lesser dresswearers replacing their rigid boning with sapling twigs or slipping it out all-together! For the first time she considered it.

Hanaan was not in the silkery, not in the gardens, not in the courtyard. When Inshik came to the dyer's courtyard, Hanaan was also no where to be seen. Another threadmaker was there in her stead. She had a wideness about her, from her flat face to her stretched mouth to her ample hips.

"Might you know where I could find Hanaan?" inquired Inshik. "She is my threadmaker."

"She will not be your threadmaker this morning. I will!"

Every thread leech stuck every one of their needle teeth into Inshik so that her dress felt as if it were sewn to her skin. Had something happened to Hanaan? Something more than falling to the ground in awe of the sky? "Is she . . . well?"

"Oh, yes," the other threadmaker said as casually as if they were talking about char beetle grinding methods. "I forgot, she told me to say that she will join you later."

The morning was spent reducing beetles to powder. The sun seemed to rise even more languidly than Inshik had that morning. When, at last, it reached overhead, Hanaan finally arrived.

"What kept you?" Inshik asked, attempting a tone of indifference.

But Hanaan only answered with: "Master Threadmaker says only squirrels tell their business to the forest."

The ceremonial spool is bequeathed to a noble lady when she becomes a dresswearer. Many a young dresswearer hopes for her first funerary mend so that she will not appear naïve, so that she might show with what grace she can carry her grief.

After she makes her first funerary rip, no dresswearer ever wishes for more.

The following day, once again, Inshik could not locate Hanaan. When the threadmaker appeared, sometime around mid-morning, it was with an equally evasive explanation as the day before. A day later, the sun had already passed its peak when Hanaan burst in. But before Inshik could attempt to again ask where she kept disappearing off to—

"Our silkies are ready to be born!" her threadmaker announced.

Their moths had been tucked away in their cocoons for one full moon cycle. Now several of the cocoons were rustling softly. Wings wakening.

"How do I tell the moth to come out?" asked Inshik, looking down at the tray of full moon cocoons.

"I will teach you the language of the silkies."

Their language was a language of air. One had to hold the egg-shaped cocoon and make the gentlest shushing at the end where the silkworm had sealed itself in. Hanaan taught her how to suck her breath in through her teeth and blow out slowly with lips pursed, then whisper a series of susurations to mimic the sound of wing beats. *Come out, little Silkie. If you come into this world gently, we will be gentle with you.*

The silk moth would unwind itself, dancing in reverse, wings unfurling as it exited through the start of the thread. Each emerged moth they transferred gently into a screened crate so that, when the moon rose, they could set the moths free by its light.

The ceremonial spool's first cut of thread is always the longest, for a dresswearer's first scars are always the grandest. She wants

to make a statement about her suffering. This is where the say-ing: "The longer the rip, the lesser the losses," originates. Though it could have just as easily been: "The smaller the rip, the greater the sorrow."

The next morning dresswearer and threadmaker began by clearing away the short outside fibers of the empty cocoons until each was as smooth as a full moon. They did this until they had a bowl mounded with cocoons. Hanaan then taught Inshik how to light a fire to boil large pots of water into which they sprinkled the little moons.

From the hole where each moth had squeezed their way into the world, Hanaan showed Inshik how to locate and tease loose the end of the silk strand. Several strands from several cocoons were needed for the one thread. Hanaan had Inshik grab a bundle (this was no easy task as the little moons bobbed and floated away at the slightest touch) and wrap the strands around a spindle carved of the same nightwood that would dye it. Near the end of each bundle, the next group of strands were twisted in, this to form one long thread, a thread that could stretch from one side of the black-spired city to the other. As she wound it around the spindle, Inshik thought of a spider she'd once watched spinning her web—back and forth, back and forth, back and forth—except instead of capturing flies, she would be capturing ghosts.

They repeated the process over many days, Hanaan and Inshik taking turns. Some days Hanaan was hard to find. Some days she was missing for half of it, arriving late or leaving early. She would only say she had other threadmaker tasks to attend to. Each night, they rested the spindle in a tray of dried rice to absorb the moisture.

"So much work for a single spool," Inshik remarked after another full day.

"Tah! Good thing there's no dressmaker here! They have to make a hundred spools for each loom."

The ceremonial spool is wound with thread made by hands that grow it, spin it, dye it and wind it, but never thread it. Nearly never.

When the last cocoon had offered its silk, they took the thread to the dyer's courtyard. Now it was their turn to stand in front of the vaporous vats.

They lit a fire of nightwood beneath and added their paste to the roiling water. First Inshik held while Hanaan dyed. Inshik observed how her threadmaker gently tugged on the single long strand to unwind it from the spindle. How she pulled it across the surface of the inky liquid, letting it dip just beneath. How she wrapped the blackened thread thumb to elbow, thumb to elbow, back and forth, back and forth.

After a while of Inshik observing, Hanaan called a couple threadmakers over to help them switch places. The threadmakers jested but Inshik did not hear what they said. Thumb to elbow, thumb to elbow, back and forth, more black thread to capture her grief with. A spider feeding on sorrow.

Once the thread was dyed night, they hung it by an open window to dry. Hanaan stepped back to admire.

"Tah, if I didn't know otherwise, I'd think this a thread-maker's work." She squeezed Inshik's arm affectionately.

Inshik felt needle teeth retract. Her lungs expanded into the space.

"Now, we will need your spool."

"My spool?"

"The empty one. In your chest. Your ceremonial spool."

Inshik had placed the chest in the corner behind the orna-mental table that held the self-renewing vase of flowers and had, wondrously, forgotten all about it.

With each step she took toward the black spool in the black casket, Inshik felt the thread teeth bite back into her breast. Hanaan was prattling away about something that Inshik could not hear over the sucking of leeches.

When they reached the room, Hanaan stuck her head out the window and whistled like a bird at some threadmakers in the garden. Inshik heard them laugh when they saw that it was her. They whistled back as Inshik crouched stiffly down beside the ornate table in her blackest dress and pulled the matching chest out from beneath it. The threadmakers continued to whistle back and forth as Inshik lifted the chest heavily beside the flowers. Suddenly, they looked like flowers at a funeral. Her joints stiffened in protest as she moved her hands to the lid of the casket and lifted it.

Inside was the threadless spool, along with the ceremonial knife for making the tear and the ceremonial needle for mending it.

The whistling was beside her. Inshik winced.

Hanaan stopped whistling mid-note.

"We don't have to wind your spool today," she said instead. "We don't even have to wind your spool tomorrow."

"But eventually we must. How much of this one will I use?" Inshik wondered aloud in a hollow voice.

"Tah, I must admit, I had never heard of someone finishing their spool before. 'Tis a lot of wounds you've had to mend."

"The spool mends the wounds in the dress, not the ones beneath it," Inshik corrected.

"Would it help to tell me about it? Master Threadmaker says that words wash away senses."

Inshik looked at Hanaan in her spring green dress. How could someone without a single scar ever understand what it felt like to be sucked dry by them? "You could never . . ."

"Tah, you think that I don't know about loss." For the first time, Hanaan's face went stony as a grave. She sat at the edge of the bed. "My brother's name was Shadiah and I had two sisters, Kial and Niak. I lost them when I came here. And a favored friend. Shini. We would sit in any tree we could climb up into, where the leaves were thick enough to be hidden from view then . . . we'd giggle! Tah, any old thing could make us giggle, especially confusing the people passing below. I still hope someone thought that we were good-natured tree sprites," Hanaan added, giggling herself. Then, abruptly, looked grave again.

"And I suppose I lost a future where I could have had a family. A hereditary one, leastwise," she added, a soft smile returning.

So Hanaan had experienced loss. But for what reason? Why would anyone willingly loose someone? "Why did you become a threadmaker?"

"Tah, I look good in green!"

Inshik knew Hanaan was joking, but she no longer felt like laughing. So Hanaan had experienced loss, she'd even taken it on willingly, but she did not carry it with her. She did not know what it was like to be weighed down by it. To wear a graveyard of grief.

Inshik closed the lid and held the casket out to Hanaan. "I am ready."

Hanaan took the chest from her hands, then set it right back down beside the flowers. "First, tell me about your mends."

Inshik startled. "Everyone wants to know, yet no one ever asks. They only whisper as I pass."

"Tah! People are noisier than stretch-snoot shrews. Well, now, I am asking."

The wearer of the blackest dress did not know how to tell Hanaan about her mends. Should she start with the worst to get it out of the way? With the least painful and ease her way in? "I do not know how to answer."

Hanaan darted over to the desk by the window and grabbed the bottle of ink and brush with the nightwood handle, long and pointed. She climbed up onto the bed and began brushing ink directly onto the white sheets.

Inshik gasped.

"We can dye it black when we're done," Hanaan dismissed as she continued painting until there was the rough shape of a dress lying on the bed. Inshik saw an outline of herself.

"Tah! Not terrible, if I so say myself."

Hanaan held the ink brush out to Inshik, but Inshik did not take it from her.

"I do not know where to begin."

"Master Threadmakers says that you have to take a first step in order to take a last one. Where did you make your first rip?" Hanaan was still holding the ink brush out to her.

Inshik took hold of the brush. She dipped it carefully into the black dye that looked like her blood. Hovered it over the heart of the bedsheet dresswearer. The ink dripped and splattered like the first drops of a downpour.

Quickly, she brushed a slash of black over the splatter.

"And why did you make it?" she heard Hanaan say.

Inshik was suddenly afraid that if she spoke she would corrupt her threadmaker's innocence. Her greenness.

"You can tell me," she heard Hanaan say in response to her hesitation.

Inshik could not look at her, not now. "This is where my favored friend drowned in our well. We were playing hawk and hare."

"Where was the next rip?" her threadmaker asked. "Draw me a map."

Inshik brushed a line of ink over the other side of the sheet.

"This where my mother reached her end. Coughing up blood."

She slashed lines all the way down one arm and then up the other.

"This is where my seminary caught fire. I was at my mother's funeral, so I was not there. Every other girl died."

Across the high neck of the jugular.

"Where my nephew perished by his own hand. He slit his throat."

She made a stroke across the stomach.

"My first stillborn."

She continued to slash the brush over the sheet, a treasure map of a thousand buried losses: "My uncle, my friend, my neighbor, my husband, my child, my second husband, my seventh child . . ."

When she was done, the sheet sagged under the wetness of the ink. Her threadmaker's face was wet as well.

"Now I will draw you *my* map," Hanaan said. She took the brush from Inshik's trembling hands, turned it around and punctured a hole into her pristine green dress. Over her heart. "This where my I will hold your grief, with you."

The ceremonial spool offers honor. For it is considered a sign of prestige for a dresswearer to remain dignified while bearing her pain so publicly.

When Inshik came to the courtyard the wide threadmaker was once again there in Hanaan's stead.

"Where is Hanaan?" inquired Inshik, not really expecting an answer. For she knew the answer. Her scars had been too dark for her green threadmaker.

"She will see you tomorrow. That's all she said I could say!"

The day was spent dipping and praying over some other wretched dresswearer's spool, but Inshik's knotted heart was not in it.

She excused herself early and lay upon the ink outline of herself, staring at the ceiling.

The ceremonial spool's sacred thread is black, for black is the color of decay and sky without sun, and under earth, and mourning. For black is the color of waking before first light and fearing what loss the new day may bring.

Inshik was woken to a cheerful knock on her door. She was still in her blackest dress, lying atop the ink-scarred sheets.

She waited the amount of time she thought it would take her to button herself into the dress. Only then did she open the door.

Hannan burst in like a warm breeze.

"Your spool is made." She handed Inshik the ceremonial chest. The black casket.

Inshik did not want to take it.

"Tah, open it!" Hanaan was bouncing on the balls of her feet.

It was not her place to argue with a threadmaker, familiar though she may be. Inshik cracked the casket.

The ceremonial spool was the size of a shin bone, wound with thread of handspun silk. Unwound, the unbroken thread would stretch from one side of the capital to the other. Only— it was not black.

Green was the color of fresh herbs and youthful nobles and the purity of threadmakers. Green was not the color of the wearer of the blackest dress.

"You have given me the wrong thread. This is a dressmaker's spool."

Inshik closed the chest and handed it back to Hanaan.

"It is the right spool." Hanaan pushed it back.

"But it is not the spool we made."

"It is the spool I made. For you." She reached over and re-opened the chest. "Every time you heal grief—a giggle, a delight, a skin-in-sun run through the gardens—you may mend over one of your black scars with this thread. And when your dress is entirely green, you can go to the Temple of the Dressmakers for a new one! Master Threadmaker says metamorphosis requires leaving the cocoons of our making."

The wearer of the blackest dress looked at the spring-green spool like she was looking at an unbroken heart. Hanaan, hopeful as spring itself in her matching dress, made this. For her. Thread that could heal the wound *beneath* the scar. With a smile, Inshik accepted her new spool.

She set the chest down, took out the ceremonial needle whittled from knot of nightwood, and threaded it green.

Master Threadmaker wore the same dress on her deathbed as that which she received upon entering the temple as a young woman, and it was nearly as green as she then had been. Spring green. Her dress bore only one single scar—a line of black across her breast—but she never said who the mend had been for until her final breath.

"It is for the wearer of the blackest dress."

LOTOPHAGE

AUGUSTO LUIZ FACCHINI

Sticky, sweaty. Lethea pushes the supply cart along the narrow corridor under the buzzing of the faltering electric light. Steam hisses from the slatted vents along the floor. Sparks from frayed wires exposed along the ceiling crackle as if in protest to the stuffy heat. Breaths in heaves. Weary aches, so heavy. She wipes her brow with her forearm, the grime of machinery grease and industrial dust blending with her damp sweat to produce a black sludge that streaks across her face like warpaint. She still remembers Omnia, still remembers Somni and little Nem, and as she levies her weight against her burden, she counts those memories, one by one, like a supplicant counting prayer beads. She whispers their names. *Omnia. Somni. Nem.* There are only 400 seconds left in her work shift. Enough time to finish two servers, if she moves quickly. Standing at the security door, she draws out the identification badge, hanging by a lanyard worn round her neck and tucked into the breast pocket of her galvanized rubber overalls, and slides it into the registry panel. Electronic beeps. Flash of green light, then a metallic hiss as the metal door slides open. The acrid smell of overheating plastic sweeps over her like a deluge pouring from a ruptured dam. Beyond the door, tubes and conduits await cleaning. She pushes her cart in and begins her labor.

"Long day?" Omnia smiles at Lethea from across the shimmering table. They're sitting on an elevated glass patio, hovering sixty meters over the shore, the placid sea washing over alabaster sand with languid tidal flows. A cool coastal wind brushes Lethea's hair, tenderly. "I'm just a little tired," Lethea says without looking. Her eyes are fixed on the edge of the horizon, the monumental clouds so clearly defined, the white birds gliding across the sky's crisp blue canvas. She can no longer recall what those birds were called.

Omnia lifts her champagne flute with her fingertips and turns her eyes to the expanse below, following Lethea's gaze.

"How much did this one cost you?" she asks then sips from the flute. Lethea turns to her and indulges in taking in Omnia's appearance: her turquoise eyes, piercing sharp. That graceful curve where her slender neck adjoins her shoulders and collarbone. Her smile, coy yet supple, gentle in the way that delicate things are. She's wearing a sparkling silver necklace that splays across the bare skin exposed by her low-cut cocktail dress. Lethea wants to remember her like this, just like this, forever.

"Don't worry about it," Lethea smiles. "It was worth it."

"It's too bad Odys isn't here to see this."

"Who?"

Omnia smiles, but her expression is laden with a sadness sweet like slow music, heavy as longing.

"Let's just enjoy this while we have it," Omnia says and turns to the shore again. The sunlight gleams on a sheen of dew over her eyes. She sips her champagne. "It's so beautiful." Lethea takes a drink from her own glass. Tasteless, tepid.

She hadn't paid for the good stuff.

Lethea removes the diodes from her temple and sits on the edge of the suspended chair inside the narrow plastic confines of the rented pod. Orange light flares in conjunction of the warbling electronic refrain: SESSION OVER. EXIT THE POD. Resting her elbows on her knees, Lethea rubs her eyes. *Who is Odys?* she wonders. She wonders how much she made from that one. Given Omnia's reaction, hopefully it was a decent amount.

SESSION OVER. EXIT THE POD.

"I know, I kn-"

SESSION OVER. EXIT THE POD.

"I KNOW the session is over!" Lethea grabs her bag and slings it over her shoulder, storming out of the little cell and into the corridor. To either side of her, along the hall, dozens of identical pods stand sentinel like ceremonial guards, most with their doors shut and a blinking red luminescent panel indicating they are in use. A junkie jostles past Lethea, nearly bowling her over, and enters the pod Lethea had just vacated. She turns to shoot a vengeful glare at whoever it was, catching a quick glimpse of a tattooed woman with varicose veins creeping spiderlike up her neck and shoulders, all skin and bones, in a dusty, ragged sweatshirt. The pod door slides shut. *I will sell you as soon as I get a chance!* Lethea mouths the words without saying them. She puts on her gas mask and heads out.

Outside, the streets seem more choked than usual, though Lethea has no frame of reference for what would be "usual" beyond more than two weeks ago. The city's denizens, in their gas masks and flimsy plastic parkas shuffle about within the press of the throng under the dark blanket of smog that obscures the upper reaches of crumbling edifices. Has the threshold of the smog layer always been this low? Lethea can't recall - certainly it seemed a little higher two weeks ago. As military drones hover past in their silent procession, neon signs flicker advertisements—cosmetics, energy drinks, neural grafts. She steps over a beggar sitting against the metal support frame that ascended to the elevated train platform overhead. Across the rusted scaffolding, spray-painted graffiti reads: *End Mnemonic Tyranny!*

"Miss, can you spare just a recollection?" the beggar mutters at her, reaching out with a pleading palm. His ribs are visible under the thin veil of flesh that stretches over his bones. He has no gas mask—just a dirty rag wound over his face. He won't last long in the smog, Lethea knows.

"Sorry," Lethea says, and tries to trudge forward into the crowd, "Good luck."

"Please miss, I don't even have my own name anymore."

Lethea clutches her plastic suit closed and tucks her head down. She forges ahead into the crowd, trying to ignore the beggar's desperate cries.

"I already had to sell my whole family—whatever family I might've had. I don't even got yesterday. Miss! Please, miss!"

"Oldest six again, right?" Lethea sits in a half-broken desk chair in the dank basement storage closet repurposed into an office. She cradles the neural extractor headband in her hands, feeling its thrumming electricity pulsating at her fingertips.

"Oldest seven," says Erisa, the property management assistant, as she clutches her smoking fentanyl cigarette with one hand and punches the keys of her terminal with the other. "*Seven*? But—"

"Rent's gone up, Lethea. They're charging oldest seven now." Erisa regards Lethea with weary eyes. There are sagging bags under them, and there's a sunken, hollow quality to them. Erisa's hair hangs to either side of her gaunt face like damp seaweed.

"But just last week I—"

"I know, I *know*. Look, I don't like it either." She takes a long drag, then exhales the smoke from her nostrils. Lethea can sense the numbing fentanyl at the edge of her skin. "You're good to wire in when you're ready."

Lethea sighs and places the headband over forehead. She closes her eyes and tries to remember, for one last time, the seventh day from oldest remaining in her memory. It was a

Saturday, she'd had to work, as usual. There was something on the news about a bombing on one of the storage servers, they said it was the Mnemonic Vanguard, a terrorist organization. Had she heard about them before? Impossible to say now if she had, those memories were long gone. She remembered she wanted to buy Omnia a gift for their anniversary, and as she was coming down the steps of the elevated train platform, she saw a holographic screen advertising a white shore beach against a serene sea, with some kind of white birds in flight under a majestic cloudscape. She remembers she stared at it for quite some time and then Everything fades. An inky blackness washes over her thoughts. She can feel the last vestiges of the memory being sucked away from her mind.

"You're all set," says Erisa. "See you next month."

The extractor's hum wanes as it powers down. She removes the headband and watches the indicator lights blink off, one by one. It doesn't matter, Lethea thinks. She still remembers Omnia, and Somni, and little Nem. That's all that matters. Those memories, she will never sell, no matter what. No matter what.

It's another day. Lethea scrubs herself with sanitary powder in the hygienic stall, pulls on her work vestments, and regards herself in the mirror. Her short black hair, clipped near bald along the sides, shows signs of ashen grey along the spots where the neural extractor's diodes hook in. Has her face always been so gaunt? She wonders if she'd looked any different a week ago.

There's a faint blue line of a varicose vein streaking like a lightning bolt from the corner of her left eye to her temple. She rubs it with the tip of her finger as though it is a smudge that will wipe off. To no avail. Has that always been there? It must have. Surely, it's normal, she decides. She pulls on her heavy gloves and buckles the suspenders on her galvanized rubber overalls. Her gas mask hangs from a cord at her neck, as she slips the clear plastic shawl over her thick clothing. She can't remember anymore why everyone has to wear these flimsy trashbag raincoats while outside—it's something to do with the radiation. But whatever it was, she sold that recollection, among a number of other critical ones, to pay for Omnia's surgery after the accident.

As she prepares herself to leave her apartment, she takes a moment by the narrow door to collect her belongings. The holographic screen over her door cycles through several product advertisements: WANT A NEW CHILDHOOD? COMPREHENSIVE GRAFTS, NO DOWN PAYMENT! — TIRED OF ITCHY SANITARY POWDERS? TRY HYPERSOL BODY GEL! — NEED CREDITS IN A HURRY? WE BUY CORE MEMORIES, CREDITS IN HAND!

Her living space is smaller than the storage closet pretending to be an office in the basement, and much of it is dominated by the side of a colossal water pipe that runs vertically from floor to ceiling, forming one of her interior walls. She can hear the constant rush of gushing water being pumped to the city's memory servers, where it serves as coolant. Soon, she will be at the heart of one of the main server vaults, scrubbing the conduits that transport this same water through the system. She wonders if she's ever felt the touch of water on her skin before. Not just the dribble from the daily water rationing, but truly *submerged* in the stuff. Like diving into that placid sea from the memory she'd bought for her and Omnia.

Suddenly, panic sparks within her before she fully knows the cause. She pats herself, reaches into her pockets. Her transport pass. It's not in her pocket where it should be. She frantically searches around the clutter on the single shelf of her dormitory—clattering a tin cup, her toothbrush, and a picture frame to the floor. Not there. She hoists herself up the short ladder to her bed, which is wedged in the tiny nook between her generator and the ceiling. She pulls the sheets and pillows, but there's nothing there either.

"No no no," Lethea cries out. There were still 160 credits on that transport pass. How is she going to get to work? "Fuck! No! No, please no!" She turns one way then another searching the floor. She ducks down onto all fours and reaches under the generator. Nothing. It's not there, and there's nowhere left to search.

"How in the hell did I get home without my transport pass?"She tries to remember what happened. Thankfully, she still had yesterday. She closes her eyes, remembering. She'd gotten off work, yes she was in a rush because she had an important date with Omnia, their anniversary. She'd taken the train, as usual, but instead of going home she'd gone into a neural graft facility — why that particular one? Maybe because it wasn't too far from her apartment building, though she couldn't say for sure anymore. She must have had her transport pass until then. So when did she lose it?

She remembered plugging into one of the immersion pods. Then there was the glass platform, the sea, the beach, the champagne that didn't taste like anything because, she reasoned, taste sensation costs extra and she must not have wanted to spare the expense. Though this was speculation—she could no longer remember having purchased the neural graft. But she must have purchased it, nonetheless.

She remembered having left the pod in a rush. She was annoyed at something. What was it? Something that happened with Omnia in the graft. Did they fight? No it didn't feel like that. Omnia had said something . . . something about . . .

Wait she felt the rush of something clicking together. There was a woman when she left the immersion pod, a cerebral junkie by the looks of her, emaciated, scrawny, webbed with blue veins. The type that will cash in even their own name for a faint recollection of joy or childhood wonder. They had bumped into each other . . .

Shit! That's where she'd lost her pass! When the junkie jostled her—she'd been pickpocketed!

"Fuck! Stupid, stupid, stupid!" Lethea jammed her feet into her boots haphazardly. She'd known about pickpockets—she'd been smart enough to keep all core memories related to safety concerns—how could she have been so foolish to fall prey to one so easily?

It had been whatever Omnia had said to her, in her

grafted memory. Something about someone else . . . Someone named . . . Tolo? Otol? What was it? She huffed as she laced her boots with reckless haste. On the floor, a framed picture had gotten knocked over, depicting a strange-looking man and a young black-haired little girl. She didn't recognize those people. She had probably known them at some point in her life, but their core memories must have been already sold. Not to worry, Lethea ventured, they can't have been that important if she had sold them. She'd never sell someone important—Omnia, Somni, little Nem. Never. No time to think about that now, she reminded herself as she slipped on her gas mask and dashed out the door.

There'd been no luck at that graft immersion place. Not that she'd expected any, who wouldn't take a free transport pass if they'd found one? She stood anxiously in line at the transport station authority at the train platform, wringing her fingers and twitching her foot as though she was in desperate need of a hygiene stall.

"NEXT PASSENGER" comes the robotic chime. Lethea lurches forward. She's already 128 seconds late to her shift.

The visage of a nondescript, bald figure regards her with expressionless eyes from within the blurry and glitchy display on the holographic screen.

"I need a transport pass, please, I—" She tries to punch the menu selections for a single round-trip pass. However, a red X appears and a computerized buzz signals an error.

"I'm afraid single round-trip passes are sold out," says the digital figure. "Would you like to buy a monthly pass for your oldest six days?"

"*SIX* days?!" Lethea cries in shock. It's *six* days now for a month's pass?

"I can't do that, I only have seven days left right now, and I still gotta buy rations—" She tries to push the single round-trip pass option again, hoping against hope for a different result.

"If there is nothing you can buy, please exit the terminal so I can assist the next passenger."

"No, please! I just need—" She looks at her watch. Already, she was now 197 seconds late. "Fuck, fuck!"

"WARNING! Agitation detected. Please purchase a pass or exit the terminal immediately. Failure to do so will result in security deployment."

Lethea looks over her shoulder in horror. She can see the hovering orbs spin in their orbits to face towards her. Indicator lights, adorning the drones' metallic surface of gyroscopic engineering like shining eyes, switch from yellow to red. She feels her guts clench, the hairs on the back of her neck prickle straight. She has a number of core memories about security drones and they are all alarming.

"Okay, okay, okay—" Lethea breathes out a whisper to the hologram. "I'll buy a month's pass." Swallowing a gulp of air, she puts on the neural extractor headband, feeling the diodes sting her temples. She closes her eyes and feels the warmth of her tears wash over her face as the machine rips six days into oblivion.

On the train ride home from work, Lethea sits with her elbows resting on her knees, her shoulders hunched, her stomach queasy. Her arms and legs feel limp and strengthless as though they're made of insulation gel. Her head throbs and swims. Dizzy. Clammy sweat. Covered in that sludge of work grime. She'd been over 386 seconds late to her workshift, which caused her pay to be docked by 90 memory credits. She'd worked four hours overtime to make up the shortfall, and skipped her rations for the day. Exhausted, Lethea stares at the floor of the train and mouthed the names. *Omnia. Somni. Nem.*

The hatch from the next car slides open and a woman wearing a long red coat and a green sash over the bottom of her face walks in.

"Fellow citizens of Djerba!" shouts the woman, reaching a gloved hand into the inside of her coat. Lethea hazily feels a tinge of fear, but fatigue overwhelms her ability to enact any response. Half-lifting her head, Lethea observes as the woman strides across the train car, throwing out small leaflets like confetti. "Do you remember who governs you?" continues the woman. "Do you remember how to vote? When all else is forgotten, try to remember this, *they* want to keep you forgetful! They don't want you to remember that it wasn't always this way! Join the Mnemonic Vanguard!"

She says the last as she exits the train car through the hatch opposite the one she'd entered from, with one last burst of little leaflets, like a priest casting a blessing upon their congregation.

No one aboard has paid the stranger any mind; the little papers fall to the floor as silently and as unperturbed as soft snow.

Lethea looks at the one pamphlet at her feet. In bright red letters, it reads: WHEN WE SELL OUR YESTERDAYS, WE LOSE OUR TOMORROW.

Alighting the train, Lethea begins descending the stairs from the platform to the street below. With every step, she aches in places she didn't even know existed on her body. She lumbers on with faltering steps, clutching the corrugated metal railing to steady herself. She feels like vomiting. Her gas mask is heavy, feels suffocating.

She stops for a moment to catch her breath. *Just gotta make it home*, she thinks. *Just make it home, then tomorrow work again. Omnia. Somni. Nem.*

She is about to resume her plodding march when her gaze falls upon a holographic billboard flashing yellow above the rising steam of massive water pipes running along the scaffolding of the train platform. In flashing letters: NEED CREDITS IN A HURRY? WE BUY CORE MEMORIES!

She stares at the sign for a long while. Then she shakes her head slightly and continues her journey home.

Incoming Neural Message.
Sender: Somni.
Message ID: 795LQXC500-V34

Source: Djerba Central Pediatric Health Facility

Hey mom, it's me. I'm guessing you aren't coming tonight any-more—is everything okay? I know I reminded you two days ago, like always. Anyway, it's Nem's birthday and I thought you were bringing us cake this year. Nem is getting real sick, worse than I've ever seen. The doctors are saying it's something with the radiation in his lungs. I know you don't remember grandpapa Odys anymore but the way Nem looks right now reminds me of him when he died. So skinny, like a bag of bones, you know? His eyes all bugging out something scary.

Anyway, my messaging allotment is almost out. Miss you, mom. I do hope you can come by the ward and see Nem, be-fore . . . well, before, you know. Bye.

Lethea sits in a reclined sofa chair under a panel of dim fluorescent light. The chamber is small, with tiled floors, dingy yellowed walls that may have once been white, with a thick, stained plastic sheet for a door. The extractor machine is much larger than any she'd seen before, and its mournful whirring and thrumming reverberate loudly in the confines of the space. A technician in a lab coat with a heavy lead vest over his chest taps onto a keyboard. "I gotta be honest, Miss Labea—"

"Lethea," she corrects him. "Sorry, Miss Lethea—there's not much else there."

"I have a bunch from work. Like paperwork and stuff. All these protocols."

"Yeah nobody wants those," the tech says, turning to her.

He's young, with a mop of curly hair and delicately cultivated facial fuzz. "Those are the kind of cores that everyone sells off first. They're not worth half-credit a dozen. I could take them like literally *all* of them, but I couldn't get you much for them. Less than a hundred. And you'd need to figure out your job all over again in my opinion, not worth it."

Lethea sighs and buries her head into her hands.

"I *could* do a nice deal for these two," the technician taps on the holographic screen, showing little yellow lines dotted across a graph.

"No, not those. I can't. Not those."

"So, the other one then?"

Lethea nods, weakly.

"Yeah?" says the tech, sliding a metallic visor over his eyes.

"Yeah." Lethea breathes out the word in a hoarse whisper, and lies back on the chair. The technician lowers an extended arm from the machine over her face and straps a cap over her forehead.

"You'll feel a slight tingle," he says.

The machine's whir elevates in pitch and volume. Lights blink on across its surface of panels and wires. The whole room lights up, blinding—then goes dark all at once.

Lethea alights the train, the bulky plastic case in her hand proving a burdensome load to negotiate through the narrow doors. Stepping aside the rush of travelers leaving and boarding, Lethea looks around to get her bearings. She must have been in this part of Djerba before, if only she could remember. Through her gas mask, she draws a deep breath, and scans the holographic signage over the framework of the station. At last seeing her destination, she cradles the case in her arms and treads across the platform towards the sign labeled *DCPHF*. Looking through the clear cover of the case, Lethea can see the silky purple cylinder, lathered with pink sauce, the words *HAPPY BIRTHDAY NEM* squirted in frosting across the top. She'd had to spend a whole day from her non-core memories on it, but it was nothing special, nothing she'd cared about losing. It was just a day at work, then meeting up with someone after. She hadn't recognized the name so she'd figured it couldn't have been anyone too important—probably just someone from work or something.

It doesn't matter, Lethea decides. As long as she still had her important core memories, that's all that matters. Somni, Nem. She'd never sell those two, no matter what.

She smiles faintly and walks towards the hospital ward.

Overhead, scrawled in haphazard graffiti, she could just make out the letters: *NEVER FORGET.*

ACKNOWLEDGMENTS

Thank you to Jake of Seedbomb for the original digital cover art. To Guiliana Keeth, our Cornell University intern and line editor on this project. To all our advanced readers. And to the writers who gave their creative energy to this anthology; may your stories live on in the memories of your readers.